Trouble Checks into Happyvale Hotel

JILL THRUSSELL

ISBN: 978-1-9999553-5-9

CONTENTS

FOREWORD

The main purpose of this book is to tell a story based loosely upon the life of Mr. Gethin and some of his experiences as the hotel manager of the Happyvale Hotel in Camden Town and it has been written on his behalf. He would like to dedicate the book to the memory of his late mother who gave him everything that she possibly could. The proceeds from this book will be used to pay debts and legal fees.

HOME SWEET ROOM THREE

For as long as I can remember the Happyvale Hotel had been my entire life, I had been born there, I'd lived there and I had even lost my virginity there, though obviously hidden well away from my mother's very watchful, Irish eyes. My mother, God bless her beautiful Irish soul had been a stern woman but quite fair and she had actually run the Happyvale Hotel single handedly whilst raising her three sons and daughter alone. A stern attitude had definitely been required however because it really wasn't easy to run a hotel in the heart of Camden, something that I would later discover throughout the course of my own adult life or even to raise three sons and a daughter singlehandedly but somehow, she had managed to battle through the financial hurdles that had often been put in her path and had soldiered on and somehow, the Happyvale Hotel had remained under her very prudent ownership.

An unorthodox approach to problems and unconventional solutions were at times, my mother's main strength and her flexible attitude, though some had called it shrewd, had somehow, over the years kept a roof over our heads and our financial boat afloat. However, I now realize as I reflect back upon those days that it might have actually been better for our family if our boat had gone on a cruise to another port entirely because the Happyvale Hotel, despite its optimistic name had never really blessed my mother in the manner that she had probably initially imagined and hoped that it would. In many respects as I look back, I now accept that the Happyvale Hotel had in fact, probably been a perpetual disappointment to my mother because she had put in so much hard work and yet had barely even managed to tread water in a financial sense. Despite the lack of financial rewards however, my mother had somehow kept her spirits high, her hotel full and she had even managed to avoid the jagged rocks of financial destitution, although the tide of poverty had threatened to rise up against the hotel's door many times and to sink our family's boat.

Quite naturally, due to Happyvale Hotel's central location and because the building itself had sat just on the cusp of Camden Town and not more than a few stone's throw away from Euston, the area and the hotel had attracted people from all walks of life which had generally gone in my mother's favor because it had meant that the hotel had not been overly reliant upon trade from tourists. Due to hotel's close proximity to the heart of the city and because Camden had always been a very popular inner-city area, many had travelled from far and wide to Camden with the hopeful wish harbored inside their minds that plentiful work could easily be secured in the city center nearby but for most, quite sadly, the reality had often fallen far short of their initial expectations and disappointment had then been their daily dish of consumption instead.

For many that had travelled to London in

those days, prior to their arrival, the city had usually been imagined to have streets paved with the promises of success and so many had sought after that success with hopeful hearts, joyful spirits and not much money inside their pockets. Since Camden had been so close to the financial pulse of the capital, it had always been one of the main boroughs in London that most people had flocked to and their first port of call as soon as they had arrived in the big city, usually penniless and often in desperate need of accommodation and so the Happyvale Hotel had in some ways, plugged that low means accommodation gap, though admittedly, not always in the most elegant manner. In some ways, my mother had really been quite fortunate because at the very least, she had owned an affordable hotel that had been situated in a prime location and as the many visitors to Camden had sought out a safe, basic place to rest their heads, my mother had answered that need although the provisions at times had been slightly strained and situated a million miles away from luxury.

The hotel that my mother had managed, owned and ran certainly hadn't been luxurious by any definition of the word but it had all belonged to her and that had been the one saving grace that had kept our family off the harsh streets and reduced the risk of potential financial destitution which had been very prevalent in those times amongst families like our own. Since Camden had always been such a densely populated, inner city area, a lot of human traffic had flowed through the borough and through the doors of the Happyvale Hotel but that continuous stream of human traffic hadn't seemed to present much of a challenge to my mother, who had always appeared to stride across life as if she had been formed and built from steel and clothed in metal armor with a shield of iron attached.

Although my mother had owned what most would consider more of a guesthouse, it had actually been named the Happyvale Hotel which had probably been her attempt to make the venue into something slightly more upmarket than financial circumstances and realities had later allowed but it had always been referred to by all who stepped across its doorstep as a hotel, possibly as a mark of respect. In so many ways, Happyvale Hotel had been a rough and ready accommodation solution to many whilst under my mother's ownership and management and whilst it hadn't provided a single shred of luxury to a single guest or conformed to what some might consider to be even the basic standards of decent accommodation, it had provided a safe place to rest your head at a price that most had been able to afford. Absolutely no one had been able to fault my mother on her hard work and continuous efforts which I had definitely appreciated and deeply respected because although she had been a stern woman and the hotel had remained at the very bottom of the hospitality ladder, she had always been an extremely hard-working individual.

My actual birth had occurred in room number six but that room had in the end, simply become the room that I had been birthed in, the place where I'd taken my first breath of life and ultimately, the place where I had released my first cry which my mother had said many times had been very loud and she had always insisted that on that day, my lungs had almost woken up the entire neighborhood. Apparently and according to my mother, my actual birth itself had been rather difficult and had actually taken hours and hours but fortunately for me, my mother had finally managed, much to her total relief I should imagine, to give birth to the life that she had carried around inside of her for nine very long months. Once born and once I had been weaned, I'd then been moved into a room just along the hallway, room number three and in that room, I had spent most of my quite mischievous childhood and all of my very adventurous, pre-adult teenage years.

On the ground floor of the building, in the hallway, a set of rules had been pinned to a notice board and very proudly displayed which had been my mother's pride and joy but the prescriptive instructions upon that notice, for the most part had been totally ignored by most of the guests who had predominantly, participated in life however they wished to and exactly as they'd seen fit. Very flamboyant breaches of those rules had really been quite frequent upon the premises itself and no daily reconciliation to each one had usually occurred because my mother had always been far too busy with incoming guests to enforce her own rigid rules very strictly, since the hotel's interior had normally been packed to the brim with human bodies which at times, had even overflowed.

Unlike some other hotels that had usually kept the staircases and halls clear and room occupancy to an agreed, fixed number of occupants per night, due to fire hazards, safety standards and so on, my mother had often allowed people to bunk down on the actual staircase and in the halls and she had even packed up to twenty people into one bedroom for the night when space had been low. The regular over occupancy of the hotel's normal capacity which had purely been motivated and indulged in due to financial pressures and various economic shortfalls however, meant that breaches of my mother's rules had been very regular, publicly flaunted and extremely obvious to anyone and everyone that had ventured inside the premises and so no one had ever really taken a single one seriously at all.

At the very rear of the building an actual garden had been situated that my mother had paid a gardener to maintain and so once a month, he had visited the hotel to tend to the area which had really been more of a yard of weeds than an organized, well-manicured greenery. Rather frustratingly for myself, throughout my teenage years, the gardener had actually become my main, male rival because I had taken a bit of a shine to one of the cleaning ladies that my mother had employed and I had regularly lusted after her but she had been far more interested in the gardener, quite naturally because he had been closer to her own age and in her sight, he'd probably been deemed to hold much more physical appeal than myself at that point in time.

Unfortunately, and much to my teenage dismay, the cleaning lady's sexual and romantic interests had clearly lain somewhere else and very securely inside the gardener's arms and that I had definitely known because he had even been caught several times in the act as he'd serviced his and her sexual requirements inside the cleaning cupboard in the downstairs basement. The mutual interest and sexual attraction between the two had been physically and sexually confirmed to me more than once and so rather reluctantly, after the third sexual occasion, I had quietly surrendered and had fully accepted defeat as I'd processed the reality because by that point, it had become extremely obvious and very clear to me that she would never be one of my sexual conquests, no matter how eagerly the passions of hot lust had pumped through my veins. When it came to the issue of the actual gardener himself, he had possessed an athletic frame with chiseled, muscular edges and so he had been a prime male specimen that had offered the cleaning lady something extremely masculine with which to quench her thirst whereas I on the other hand, at that time, had just been a skinny, puny teenager with a lustful crush and sexual desires that would never be satisfied, or at least not by her.

Despite the cleaning lady's lack of sexual interest in me however, I had still optimistically managed to make the most of her presence and my time around her and every now and then I had managed to enjoy a sneak peek of her cleavage which had offered me an image to recall and reminisce upon later at night and discreetly provided me with some imagery for my own sexual fantasies. The images that I had kept inside my mind of her exposed body parts, had allowed me to see her naked and be intimate with her many times in a nonphysical sense without her actual involvement, knowledge or her even participation and that had in the end, at least managed to satisfy me to some degree.

On a several occasions and whenever I had felt particularly bold, I had even requested that the cleaning lady in question clean certain areas or perform certain tasks, just to see if I could catch a quick glimpse of her thighs and cleavage which would then be exposed and on show. Such opportunities however, really hadn't presented themselves to me very often because the cleaning lady had adhered to a very strict cleaning routine that had to be performed every working day and she had followed that schedule almost religiously, except on the occasions when she'd been busy down in the basement with the gardener.

When it came to the actual overnight guests that had occupied the guest rooms and at times, even the staircase and halls, my mother hadn't been particularly fussy and as long as you had been able to pay for your night's stay up front, you would have been welcomed in and then given a roof over your head. For some my mother's hotel had been a place where they had always felt very welcome and quite comfortable, despite its material shortfalls because she had accepted many into its confines without judgement, prejudice or discrimination as long as they could pay the going nightly rate and as long as when they stayed, they didn't cause any boisterous drama or any noisy fuss.

Several guests and their period of occupancy at the hotel had been slightly more permanent in nature and they had stayed in the building for quite long periods of time and they would usually be referred to as 'Resies' and those long-term residents had always been given their own rooms. Unlike the casual overnight guests, the Resies had never been asked to share their rooms and they had generally been treated with much more respect due to their more permanent occupancy. The packed in sardine tin experience had usually only applied to short term and casual overnight guests and since my mother hadn't liked to turn either guests or money away, at times the human overflow had been physically hard to maneuver around because the human bodies had often spilled out into the halls and overflowed onto the staircase.

Animals had never been permitted to enter or allowed anywhere inside the premises by my mother but if any had dared to venture into that crowded space on a sardine packed night, they probably would have dashed straight back out of the hotel's front door again within minutes because hygiene it appeared, hadn't really been a top priority for some of the packed in overnight guests. The collective sweatiness of the human overflow had at times emitted, a very sour, powerful aroma and that bitter aroma had sometimes been quite difficult for human nostrils to cope with but my mother had never swayed or deviated from the compromises that she had deemed to be necessary for our and the hotel's financial survival.

Almost every kind of person imaginable had

stepped foot inside the Happyvale Hotel and had stayed inside the building throughout my mother's reign and she had welcomed anyone and everyone as long as they had the financial means to stay and then she had settled them down for the night wherever she could find a space large enough for them inside our humble abode. Although the Happyvale Hotel had never quite managed to become the luxury, upmarket kind of hotel that my mother had probably hoped at one time that it might be, it had housed years of drama, countless nights of shenanigans and plentiful days of chaos inside its walls and that had at least, provided me with years of amusement and with some very funny memories to reflect upon, from the years of my youth. Many of my days had been spent throughout my childhood and teenage years in the throngs of that chaos and as I had mingled with some of the guests and entertained myself inside the halls which had been filled with dramatic shenanigans, regretful tears and rambunctious laughter, the walls and halls of the hotel had aged over the years alongside me. Somehow however and despite everything, almost miraculously, the Happyvale Hotel had quite remarkably and probably due to my mother's prudent attitude and shrewd approach to life, always remained our main family home throughout my entire childhood years.

Aside from my lustful desires for one of the cleaning ladies, the many guests that had occupied the hotel had regularly provided me with a source of entertainment because practically every day, something chaotic and dramatic had occurred that had revolved around their occupancy and the hotel's meagre accommodation provisions. A few of the guests that had occupied a guest room in the hotel during my mother's ownership had left quite an impression upon me during the years of my youth, mainly due to their quirky characters, unorthodox approach to life or perhaps even just because of their strange attitudes towards others, the hotel itself or towards life in general and some memories of those very memorable people still remain with me until this very day.

Sometimes even now, I still wonder what became of some of the guests that had left a memorable footprint inside my memories and a distinct impression imprinted upon my mind during my mother's reign over Happyvale Hotel, once they had left my mother's walls permanently behind because they had truly been such an integral part of my youth. One of the male guests that I had admired the most, especially throughout my teenage years, had always been Ralphie the Rogue and his nickname which had been given to him by some of the female guests at the hotel had suited him right down to the ground and although he hadn't been a permanent guest, every six months or so he'd stayed in London at the hotel for a few weeks when back on shore because he had been a sailor.

Apparently, in every city and port that Ralphie the Rogue had visited on the crest of his roguish wave, from what he had often related to those around him and I had managed to overhear, there had been a lady in waiting and usually more than one because they had rarely waited around long enough for his usually quite brief returns to solid land. In fact, by the time Ralphie had usually, finally returned to the city in question for a second round of skinny dips in each ladies sea of passion, the women had usually moved on to far greener love pastures and much brighter, more solid romantic prospects and they had even entered into committed relationships with other men that had been far more accessible to them and men that would have given Ralphie a skinful, if he'd even tried to have another roll in the hay with them.

Many of my evenings and nights had however, been spent huddled up in a corner of the ground floor hotel hallway with my ears and a glass to the wall, or sprawled out upon the floor of a room next to a cracked doorway as I had listened to Ralphie the Rogue's tall, seductive tales which had usually been related to some of the other male guests at the hotel. Each tale had revolved around one of Ralphie's sexual conquests and had usually been told after the consumption of a few glasses of whiskey and he had worn each one like a medal of honor as he'd verbally boomed every juicy detail triumphantly to his audience of male peers and orally displayed each one to convince those around him of his manly achievements. Much like a trophy of bravery that had been earned at sea, Ralphie the

Rogue had orally displayed his sexual conquests to any adult male that would listen but in this instance, his display case had been his mouth and his trophies had been the women that he had managed to convince to hop into bed with him and since I had lacked such highly desirable interactions with the female species at the time, I'd been extremely impressed by his masculine prowess and seemingly, plentiful sexual achievements.

Prior to my teenage years, from what I can remember, Ralphie the Rogue had occupied a room at the hotel for a few weeks at a time roughly twice a year and he had at times brought us little gifts from lands far and wide which he had then proudly presented to us in front of our mother. When Ralphie's gifts had been given to us, he had then usually tussled our hair in a fatherly manner and it had almost felt as if he had wanted to impress my mother for one reason or another. In my late teenage years and as I had grown older, I'd often secretly wondered if perhaps Ralphie the Rogue had wanted my mother to be a lady in waiting at one of his ports but my tongue and lips had never allowed me to present that question to either party because I had definitely feared a verbal lashing from my mother's razor, sharp tongue and possibly more from Ralphie himself and I'd wanted to live to see and enjoy my own adult years.

One of my most treasured memories of a guest that had resided at the hotel when my mother had been in control of the building, has always been Mavis for more reasons than one because she had truly been an arm of support and a friendly hand of comfort to me during my younger, very curious, childhood years. Almost every day that Mavis had occupied a guest room, she had greeted me with a warm friendly smile and a small chocolate gift in a silver wrapper and she'd even gone out of her way to converse with me quite regularly which had been something that the majority of the guests had never bothered to do because in those days, children had to generally be seen and not heard and had only been permitted to speak directly to adults, if they had been personally invited to.

Unlike some of the other guests however, Mavis who had been in her late fifties, from what I can remember, although her age had been something that I had never dared to ask and a widow had always taken a little time out of her day to hold a conversation with me and she had frequently, patiently listened to some of my issues in life. At that time, my issues in life had predominantly revolved around arguments with my peers and disputes with my siblings and so she had often offered me snippets of wisdom to guide me and chunks of advice to assist me as I had attempted to navigate my way through the slightly rocky terrain of childhood and the quite perilous mountains of my early teenage years.

On occasions, Mavis had even encouraged me to have some kind of aspirations in life and those motivational words of encouragement had accompanied the chocolate treats like drops of comfort that soothed my ears and mind because not many people had ever really given a dam about whether or not I had ever aspired to achieve anything in life and certainly not any of the other guests at my mother's hotel. In those days because chocolate had generally been regarded as a special treat, it had not been something that any child had expected to consume every single day or even very frequently but when Mavis had been around that luxury had been offered to me almost as often as my daily evening meals which had usually consisted of Irish stews, various hearty, pulse laden broths, potatoes and dumplings. The chocolate treats however, had always been considered far more delicious by my young palate and deeply appreciated because Mavis had been the only person that ever gave me such luxuries on a regular basis.

Sometimes on Saturday afternoons, when I had taken a wander out into the garden at the rear of the hotel, I'd often found Mavis seated upon a wooden tree stump that had barely stood taller than the weeds that had surrounded it and she had related some of her memories to me about the life that she had once lived and shared by her late husband's side. Everything that Mavis had told me, from what I can remember had utterly intrigued me not necessarily because it had been full of excitement but simply because she had taken the time to discuss some of the complexities of life with me and those discussions had given me an understanding to some extent about what adult women usually expected from the adult men that they loved.

Unfortunately however, when I had reached the tender age of about twelve, Mavis and my mother from what I had been able to grasp from the snippets of conversations that I'd overheard at the time that I had not really been supposed to hear, had a huge fall out possibly due to some kind of financial dispute and so she had packed up her small suitcase and then had left the hotel immediately, rather abruptly one evening. After that day, very sadly, Mavis had simply never ever actually returned and deep down inside, I still feel that some part of me had left with her that day because no other guest during the time of my mother's ownership or even my own had ever touched my heart in quite the way that Mavis had.

Despite my deep respect for Mavis and my slightly misguided admiration for Ralphie the Rogue, a couple of other guests at the hotel during the time of my mother's ownership had left their impressions upon me for entirely different reasons and not all of them had been pleasant or even remotely positive. A couple of the guests had somehow, even become my enemies over the years in various ways because they had either done things that I hadn't liked or they had disliked me intensely and overtly shown it. One such hugely disliked but definitely very memorable guest had been Fishy Frank who had always stunk of fish because he had worked in a fishmongers and each time I had encountered him, in the hotel halls or upon the staircase, the usual response from Frank had been a hateful sneer and at times, he'd even brandished his descaler inside one of his hands like some kind of weapon and had then shaken it at me. Since I had not been the bravest of chaps and certainly hadn't fancied being descaled by him, on the occasions when he had taken out his descaler, I had fled almost instantly and had found any safe corner to hide in that had been close by, if access to my own room had been blocked by his person at the time.

Rather frustratingly and quite annoyingly, Fishy Frank had been one of my mother's most highly treasured guests throughout his period of residence, since he had been a worker and a very reliable, consistent payer and so my mother had always discouraged any displays of rudeness towards him or any kind of disrespect. Occasionally however, if Fishy Frank had walked away from me and I hadn't seen the descaler, I'd cast an angry scowl towards him and wave a brave fist at his back but such offensive gestures and faces I had never dared to boldly present to his face because if Fishy Frank had caught me, he'd probably have complained to my mother within two seconds flat and then I would have gone without dinner and would have had to eat bread and butter for at least a month.

In those days, the punishments that mother had normally inflicted upon me had varied but usually, if I had been caught in a moment of naughtiness and direct rudeness, I'd have just bread and butter for dinner for a while and for me that sacrifice, just for a few seconds of glory, I had definitely felt at the time hadn't been worth it. Once or twice I had mentioned Fishy Frank's descaler to my mother but she had always just advised me very sternly to stay out of his way and not to cause any trouble with any of the guests and especially not with those who paid a decent rate for their accommodation and those who paid on time.

"Frank pays well and he pays on time, so Steven you mustn't bother or upset him because a sure penny is better than an empty room." My mother had instructed me on several occasions in a very stern, firm tone. "Empty rooms mean empty stomachs."

Quite unfortunately, since I hadn't been in the financial position to offer my mother any kind of compensation for the loss of income that she might have had to suffer, if I had stood up to Frank and upset him, I'd simply had to swallow my pride and accept his displays of anger but I had usually kept as far away from him as I possibly could to avoid any kind of trouble. Since at that point in time, I had already had several very negative run-ins with Fishy Frank, I'd learnt to totally avoid him whenever I had noticed him and to immediately turn and walk in the opposite direction because it had seemed like the wisest thing to do, if I'd wanted to stay in my mother's good books and in order not stir up any upset because that upset, would have definitely provoked her anger which would have then been taken out on me in the form of a punishment.

When it had come to the actual issue of female companionship, I had noticed that Fishy Frank absolutely never ever had any kind of female companion on his arm, unlike Ralphie the Rogue who had it seemed, been able to attract women with total ease due to his magnetic charm, athletic frame and rugged good looks. Throughout my younger years although I hadn't really questioned the reasons behind that feminine absence in Fishy Frank's life, as I'd leapt into my teenage years I had finally attributed his lack of appeal to the stench that had accompanied him everywhere he had gone and his sneery stares which had usually taken one of several forms, all of which had been unsightly at best and totally repulsive at worst.

Although Fishy Frank had been greatly disliked and totally avoided by myself, he hadn't however been the most disliked guest that I had encountered throughout my mother's period of ownership of the Happyvale Hotel and there had been several other guests that had been far worse, one of whom had been

Snide Stuart. The nickname Snide Stuart which I had quite proudly, given to him myself actually suited him right down to the ground because he had a snide side to his character that had made trouble wherever he had placed his feet. For the sake of my own self-preservation, I had learnt very quickly to totally avoid Snide Stuart because he had been absolutely horrible and, on several occasions, he had even complained to my mother about me with wild accusations, twisted facts, total lies, warped distortions and derogatory exaggerations and so I'd steered well clear of him.

On one such occasion I had been outside in the back garden one evening engaged in a game that I'd often played where I had knocked empty cans of the top of a tree stump with small stones and Snide Stuart had come outside and had then walked around the tree stump whilst I'd been in the midst of my game. Since one of the small stones had hit Snide Stuart's leg, totally accidentally, he had then angrily flown straight back into the hotel and had told my mother that I had thrown an actual stone at him which I most certainly hadn't. Due to Snide Stuart's false accusations however, I had then gone without my evening meal and been given nothing but bread and butter to eat for dinner for the rest of that entire week.

After several run-ins with Snide Stuart which had always resulted in the loss of my evening meals for at least a week, I had then avoided him almost like the plague and if I had seen him anywhere, be it in the garden, inside the hotel halls or even upon the staircase, I had quickly fled to the safety of my room and had hidden myself from his sight. Somehow, Snide Stuart had a way of making everything appear to be my fault and it had almost been as if he had deliberately sought out any trouble that he had been able to find with me on whenever the opportunity had presented itself to him.

Since Snide Stuart had been an adult, he had always managed to convince my mother that I had been in the wrong and then I'd taken the blame and the punishment that she had dished out to me afterwards, every single time and so due to his trouble making and hateful attitude towards me, I had absolutely loathed him. When it had come to my mother's actual attitude towards Snide Stuart, on the other hand, he very much like Fishy Frank had been another consistent payer that had paid a decent rate and so I had been advised to steer well clear of him and not to speak to him at all and after a few very negative run-ins with him and the loss of my evening meals on several occasions, I'd fully surrendered in total defeat and then hidden from him as much as I had physically been able to.

Much later on in life however, I had finally realized the grim reality of my mother's actual existence, especially when it had come to the issue of guests like Fishy Frank and Snide Stuart in that no matter how horrible, nasty, rude or offensive someone had or hadn't been, if they had paid a decent rate, had paid consistently and had been financially reliable, they had been accommodated and provided with a courteous service. Curtesy according to my mother's instructions and rules had to be extended towards all guests at all times and even to those that hadn't seemed to deserve it which had meant, no matter how antisocial, disrespectful or ill-mannered a guest had been that curtesy had to be shown and extended towards them. Somehow and despite all the odds, my mother's strict instructions and rules had managed to keep several very difficult guests at the hotel for many years, irrespective of their total disregard for those around them and their extremely, unpleasant, antisocial attitudes but as I now reflect, I truly realize and appreciate that to retain such a tolerant attitude, must have been a very hard, bitter pill of humility for her to have to swallow every single living day and night but she had done so with a smile on her face and her held high.

STATUS NO QUO

Nothing beyond the front doors of the Happyvale Hotel had ever been the same from one day to the next and the fluctuations in events, guest occupancy, drama and chaos had really kept my mother on her toes because some of the things around us had changed continuously. One day there might have been a chaotic storm of upset and the next day an influx of hilarity and drama as the shenanigans of the guests had decorated the internal walls of the hotel with as much headache, heartbreak, joy, pain and laughter as they had been able to fit into every single living day and night.

Most of the hotel's guests however, despite

the chaotic shenanigans, at least had a respectful attitude towards my mother because if anyone had dared to upset or offend her personally, they would have been quickly shown the door and have been rapidly booted out. Although patience hadn't been a quality that my mother had adorned her interior with in abundance that lack had actually suited the Happyvale Hotel quite well because it had been situated in the heart of Camden which had been the jungle of rough edges around the fringes of the more refined city center. Fortunately for our family however, my mother had been a tough cookie made from the dough of sternness and her tough makeup had definitely been required to keep both the hotel and us financially afloat. Since the hotel had been situated very close to the city center, it had attracted all kinds of people inclusive of some lowlife and so my mother's zero tolerance, no nonsense attitude had protected us all to some extent, had kept the hotel's doors open and had even saved her from tons of headache but now as I reflect, I realize that it had been a very hard slog for her through a valley of stress and that there really had been very few peaks of joy.

Although there had been several long-term guests that had stayed at the hotel for years and years, there had also been a consistent flow of short terms guests that had stayed for a night, a week, a fortnight or sometimes even up to a month and many of those temporary guests had been a regular source of amusement to me that had provided me with quite generous daily portions of hilarity. Quite often clashes had occurred between some of the more permanent guests and the short-term guests since the latter had been far less bothered about the maintenance of any pleasant long-term relationships with other occupants which had meant, they had willingly littered the hotel's hallways with drama, shenanigans and with far less restraint.

On several occasions, much to my total delight, some of the permanent guests that I had absolutely loathed, like Snide Stuart and Fishy Frank had even been taken down a peg or two by those temporary visitors that my mother had usually referred to as tourists. The tourists had normally occupied a guest room on the premises for a short period of time after their initial arrival but that nickname hadn't meant that they had been on vacation from another place and they had predominantly for the most part, usually just been fortune seekers in search of a better life on the streets of the capital city.

Due to the nature of the tourist's short-term visits and the suitcases full of drama that some of them had brought along with them, they had at times livened up my days and nights and, on some occasions, I had even rejoiced as they had taken on my enemies directly such as Snide Stuart and Fishy Frank. The status quo had often been challenged by some of these larger than life personalities and to watch my enemies squirm at times as they had been dealt some very harsh, direct blows of humiliation, drama and headache due to some of the tourist's chaotic antics, I have to admit had thrilled me to some extent.

In some ways, the chaotic antics, verbal blows and various challenges that the tourists had dealt and presented to my enemies had almost felt like a form of compensation to me, for the many evenings of bread and butter that I'd had to endure as a form of punishment because of guests like Fishy Frank and Snide Stuart, both of whom I had absolutely loathed. Just to see some of those obnoxious bullies be nailed down to the ground with trouble as they had faced and come up against troublemakers that had been far better equipped to handle them than myself had given me some small grains of comfort at times and those joy filled moments had managed to slightly appease me, even though I had not been personally involved in any of tourist's triumphant victories.

On one such occasion I remember that Snide Stuart had picked on a woman in her mid-sixties, who unlike most of the other tourists had been an actual tourist on vacation that had taken a trip to London to see some of her family members that had lived in the capital city. Apparently, the woman had wanted to make something to eat in the kitchen before she went out one evening to see her family and Snide Stuart had obstructed her from doing so for almost an hour as he had hogged the entire kitchen and the cooker rings all to himself.

Rather frustratingly for the woman, Snide Stuart had refused to give her any kind of access to even a ring of heat on the small cooker inside the shared guest kitchen and as I had watched them both from the hallway, the sands of her patience had finally run out and then some impatient words had flown directly from the woman's mouth. Although the tone of woman's questions had been quite short, curt and sharp, she had simply asked Snide Stuart how much longer he would be and if he planned to be much longer because she had a special outing to attend that evening. True to Snide Stuart's usual rude, obnoxious self however, he had immediately retorted with insults and then he had even slammed things down on the kitchen worktop just before he had proceeded to storm around the interior of the quite small kitchen.

Unfortunately, in the midst of Snide Stuart's rant and temper tantrum, somehow, he had actually managed to bump into the woman physically and then suddenly, all hell had broken loose as she had, much to my total delight, started to thump him over the head with her handbag and had yelled some insults at him at the top of her voice. Just a few seconds later the situation had escalated even further as I had watched in fascinated silence as the woman had picked up some of Snide Stuart's cooked food which had been placed upon a plate on top of the kitchen worktop next to the cooker and then she'd proceeded to tip the entire contents of his plate all over the kitchen floor.

Very shockingly indeed, in direct response to the woman's actions, Snide Stuart had then rapidly stormed towards the woman and had even tried to grab her arm before she could do any more damage to his potential evening meal as I had stood and watched him in total horror. However, and perhaps quite luckily, in the midst of all that chaos Snide Stuart had somehow managed to slip upon some of the food on the kitchen floor and so he had then ended up upon the ground on his backside and the woman, whose arm he had actually managed to grab by that point, had quickly ended up in a heap directly on top of him.

Since the mature female guest had already dealt with Snide Stuart that evening to some extent and had not only given him a few good wallops with her handbag but had also dealt him some very stiff, razor sharp words of verbal humiliation which I had hoped would force him to take a step towards decency, I'd decided at that point to notify my mother before the situation erupted into a full-scale fist fight. A definite fear had lurked inside my mind at the time that at any given moment, if I had said nothing at all, there might have been an actual physical fist fight and so once I'd scurried along the hallway of the hotel's ground floor, I had then rapidly knocked upon my mother's door and she had immediately responded as she'd quickly opened up the door, listened to me for a few seconds and then grabbed her keys from the nail hook beside the door. Just a couple of seconds later my mother had swept out of her room, slammed the door shut behind her and then she had stridden briskly down the hallway towards the kitchen that adjoined the lounge.

"What on earth is going on in here?" My mother had demanded as she had stepped into the lounge and had confronted the two guests.

"He wouldn't let anybody else use the cooker Mrs. Gethin." The woman had rapidly replied. "I've waited for over an hour and I have theatre tickets for this evening that I've already paid for."

"Is this true Stuart?" My mother had asked.

"I was just cooking my evening meal like I always do." Stuart had replied with a shrug. "She never even asked me, she just started having a go at me."

"I only asked you a couple of questions and you've hogged all the dam rings for the past hour." The woman had swiftly snapped back. "Every single one of them and when I confronted you about it, you insulted me and then threw a temper tantrum."

"Stuart, you have to share the kitchen and she is a lady which means, you have to be a gentleman." My mother had gently reminded him.

Once my mother had calmed the situation down and we had left the kitchen with the female guest, my mother had then sent me to bed before she had returned to her room with the female guest in tow who she'd promised could access the hotplate warmer in her room. My mother's room had been very self-sufficient in that it had composed of a bedroom area, an adjoined kitchen and lounge and in one corner of the room there had even been a small, compact office of sorts and inside that space, she had performed most of the tasks that hotel ownership and her family responsibilities had required on a daily basis and whilst it hadn't been the height of luxury, it had definitely sufficed and had made our lives slightly easier.

Several regrets had lingered in my mind however, as I had left the female guest in my mother's safe hands and then had begun to walk along the hallway towards my room, all of which had all revolved around Snide Stuart and the events of that evening. A rather mischievous notion had tugged away inside my thoughts as I had entered inside my room and then prepared to rest for the night as I'd silently considered the possibility that perhaps I should have allowed the disagreement between Snide Stuart and the female guest to continue and escalate into an actual physical fight. If Snide Stuart had intentionally struck the lady physically, quite possibly, my mother would then have had to kick him out of the actual hotel forever and so rather unintentionally that night, it suddenly dawned upon me that through my intervention, I had actually saved Snide Stuart's obnoxious backside from a possible eviction and that one outcome, I'd definitely regretted at the time.

Only one small comfort had really remained for me that night in the midst of that very awful realization as I had lain down upon my bed and then prepared to sleep and that had been the fact that at least there hadn't been a full-scale fist fight because then the female guest might have actually been injured. Despite my failure to make the most of an opportunity to eradicate Snide Stuart from my environment forever however, a huge dollop of satisfaction had begun to comfort my mind as I had started to rest and that slightly satisfactory outcome had related to Snide Stuart himself in that for the very first time ever, my mother had seen with her own two eyes the kind of person that he had really, actually been.

Although the increase in my mother's awareness when it came to the issue of Snide Stuart's character and nature had been considered a slight improvement, when it had come to my own position as I had also known at the time, it hadn't been a total guarantee that I'd never be punished again due to Snide Stuart's antagonistic provocation. One silver lining had however, accompanied that particular cloud of dismay and although that cloud had dampened my mood and spirit to some extent as I had closed my eyes, I'd managed to find a small grain of comfort in the knowledge that in some small way that evening, I had been slightly vindicated by Snide Stuart's actions in my mother's sight. Due to the damage that had been delivered to Snide Stuart earlier that evening via the woman's wallops with her handbag and her verbal insults, my mind had felt slightly satisfied as I had managed to retain a small spark of hope that Snide Stuart might be slightly less awful towards me in future, a prospect which had at the very least, slightly appeased me and so that night, I'd managed to drift off into the gentle arms of slumber reasonably peacefully.

The worst run-in at the hotel however, that had involved a tourist and that had revolved around the kitchen had not related to Snide

Stuart at all and had in fact, involved Fishy Frank who had been up in arms one day because some food items of his that he had just cooked had actually gone missing when he had returned to his room to collect something. Apparently, Fishy Frank had prepared a very expensive steak with some new potatoes and veg which he had already stuck upon a plate and then he had left his evening meal unattended for a couple of minutes as he had returned to his room to collect something.

Since Fishy Frank had worked for an actual fishmonger, he had usually sourced all his evening meals from work free of charge and so predominantly, his dict had usually contained a generous helping of fish every day, on this particular occasion however, a prime piece of steak had been specially purchased and then had been eagerly prepared for his consumption. Due to the expensive outlay in comparison to Fishy Frank's usual evening meals, he had therefore been extremely enthusiastic to enjoy that very rare treat and to savor the meaty, chunk of flesh when he consumed it.

Upon Fishy Frank's hungry return to the kitchen and his subsequent angry discovery, namely the absence of his evening meal, his temper had then immediately flared and sparks of anger had flown from his eyes as he had stormed around the ground floor of the hotel in a fit of absolute rage. At the time I had been situated in the hallway quite close to the kitchen door and so I'd quickly hidden from sight since I had known that Fishy Frank had a very nasty temper but I'd still kept him in my sights, purely because anything that had annoyed Fishy Frank had been perceived as a potential source of amusement for me, simply because I had absolutely loathed him.

Just a few minutes later I had watched in total silence as Fishy Frank had stormed out into hallway and then he had begun to search the interior of the hotel high and low for the guilty party but there had been absolutely no one to be seen on the ground floor, on the hotel staircase or inside any of the communal bathrooms. Once Fishy Frank had finished his inspection of the interior of the hotel, he had then walked briskly towards the back door and the back garden and as he'd headed out towards the shed, I had started to follow him outside just to satisfy my own curiosity. In so many ways, Fishy Frank's anger had definitely amused me and since on this occasion, his anger hadn't actually been directed towards me, I had felt a curious urge to see what might happen next because Fishy Frank had possessed a turbulent nature and his temper had always been extremely volatile which had meant, his reactions could be very unpredictable.

Unfortunately for the thief, he had decided to hang out and actually consume Fishy Frank's evening meal inside the actual shed and so as soon as Frank had opened up the shed door, he had caught the thief red-handed with a forkful of food raised to his lips. Since the shed door had remained open I had actually been able to see Fishy Frank as he had grabbed the man by the scruff of the neck and had then pulled him to his feet and although it had amused me at the time that Fishy Frank had absolutely hit the roof, I'd also begun to fear for the other man's safety. In terms of Fishy Frank's build and stature, he hadn't been a slim man and he had actually been rather chunky and overall, he'd possessed a very muscular frame and so I had worried at that time that the other male guest might be beaten to a pulp in just a few minutes because Fishy Frank had looked angry enough to deliver that kind of physical damage.

Before Fishy Frank could actually, physically demolish the man however, I had rapidly made a decision and then I had run back inside the hotel and through the main ground floor hallway and had knocked very loudly upon my mother's door and after a few brief seconds, she had responded. A few rushed explanations had fallen from my lips and tumbled from my mouth just before my mother had hurriedly begun to rush through the ground floor hallway towards the back garden and towards Fishy Frank. Since I had been extremely interested in any kind of annoyance that had bothered Fishy Frank and I'd wanted to ensure that my mother would be alright, I had immediately begun to follow my mother as I'd rushed down the hallway behind her and then out into the back garden.

Once my mother had arrived beside the

open shed door, she had then stood beside the door as she'd begun to address Fishy Frank boldly and directly as she had immediately tried to pour some words of calmness onto the fiery scene in an attempt to calm Fishy Frank and the situation down.

"Frank, what in heaven's name is going on?" My mother had asked.

"This little runt stole my plate of food from the kitchen Mrs. Gethin." Frank had immediately replied. "And so, I'm just about to knock ten bells out of him."

"Right Mr. Mekkle, you'll have to reimburse Frank for the food that you took and you should apologize to him immediately." My mother had insisted.

"Okay." Mr. Mekkle had replied. "I'm sorry."

"Sorry, sorry doesn't give me my dam dinner back." Frank had barked.

"I'll have to go and get my wallet, it's in my room." Mr. Mekkle had rapidly pleaded as a sheepish expression had crossed his face.

"Okay Mr. Mekkle, you'd better go and do that immediately." My mother had advised. "I'll come with you."

Upon Fishy Frank's face there had been a look of total thunder as he had watched Mr. Mekkle and my mother as they had vacated the shed and then had headed back towards the back door of the hotel and although the situation had been handled to some extent by my mother's wise hands, I had been under absolutely no illusions at all at the time that his thunderous mood might fully erupt at any given second. Due to Fishy Frank's anger at that point, I had wisely decided to retreat to the safety of my own room as quickly as possible because I had absolutely no desire whatsoever to cross Fishy Frank's path when his temper had recently been ignited, shaken and had even erupted, due to any fiery hot sparks and overspills of angry lava that might possibly fly or flow in my direction. Since Fishy Frank and I had always been sworn enemies, I'd definitely felt that a quick departure had been absolutely necessary, purely for the sake of my own self-preservation and so I had immediately abandoned any further curious explorations of his rage and had hurriedly scarpered back to the sanctuary of my own room.

Quite unusually, one day however, Ralphie the Rogue had also crossed paths with trouble throughout one of his short, quite brief stays at the hotel but unlike Fishy Frank and Snide Stuart that trouble had been in full alignment with Ralphie the Rogue's usual nature and had pretty much been self-inflicted. In accordance and in full alignment with Ralphie the Rogue's lustful appetite for the female gender, quite naturally that trouble had of course involved a woman, or more specifically, one of the men that one of his female lovers had entertained.

Since Ralphie the Rogue had once more stepped foot upon dry land near the city, his first port of call had quite naturally of course been the hotel to book a room for a few weeks and then he had immediately paid a hopeful visit to one of his ladies in waiting. However, this particular woman had been tied up in some kind of romantic knot with another man at the time and although the two hadn't been married and the man hadn't actually been present during Ralphie's visit, he had taken offence to

Ralphie's infringement upon his sexual territory and so, he had then sought Ralphie out and had even come to the hotel to actually find him.

Prior to the man's arrival at the hotel's front door, I had actually been in the guest lounge with Ralphie and we had been in the midst of a discussion because I'd liked to be around Ralphie and at times, he had taken the time to converse with me when he hadn't been otherwise engaged. Unlike some of the other guests, Ralphie hadn't seemed to mind my presence and sometimes, he had even advised me about the ways of the world and the women that lived inside it which along with his interest in me had hugely impressed me throughout my early teenage years. So quite often, whenever Ralphie had been on dry land and not otherwise engaged with one of his ladies, I had spent some time with him in the evenings and I'd listened to him speak as he had drunk a whiskey or two inside the lounge.

On this particular occasion however, a loud knock had suddenly been heard by us both at the front door and Ralphie, since the lounge had been situated quite close to the front door, had immediately responded as he had stood up and then had actually gone to answer it himself. No sooner had Ralphie opened the front door however, and faced the man who had not actually been known or recognizable to him at the time, then some angry sparks had rapidly flown in Ralphie's direction from a very angry male. Much to my absolute horror, as I had heard some raised voices at the front door and had then followed Ralphie out of the lounge, from the top of the hallway I'd seen Ralphie be dragged down the hotel's front steps by the man as Ralphie's apologetic explanations had fallen upon deaf ears.

Although Ralphie's physical frame had been quite strong, his opponent had either been far stronger or perhaps had just been angrier and so he had managed to wrestle Ralphie to the ground and even had him held him a head lock in just a matter of minutes. Since I hadn't been physically equipped to assist Ralphie in any capacity, I'd quickly turned around and then rushed towards my mother's room door in order to seek her assistance because I had generally only regarded bravery to be a useful quality when victory looked remotely possible and in that instance, defeat looked like the only, highly probable outcome when it came to the issue of my potential physical interference and so, I'd very wisely, hastily retreated.

Despite the fact that my mother hadn't been very physically powerful and especially not in comparison to some of the men that I had seen her stand up to over the years, she had possessed a razor-sharp tongue, a stubbornly stern attitude and an extremely loud voice and all of those three characteristics combined had presented a strong wall of opposition, when and if required. In fact, my mother's approach towards difficult people and the way she had tackled difficult situations, now that I reflect, in many ways had seemed almost miraculous because she had been able to calm down an angry, aggressive situation in a matter of minutes with just one verbal lash or one wise rebuke from her tongue.

Much to my absolute and total relief, once my mother had responded to my pleas for assistance and she had arrived beside the front door, the two men had then immediately paused mid-action and had turned to face her. Due to the explosive current of anger between the two men, I had remained close to the front door and although I'd not stepped foot outside, I had been able to hear my mother's voice as she had addressed both men and as she'd swiftly shut down the angry, explosive physical outburst between them both.

"Right gentlemen, if you are going to have a fist fight, you'll need to do that somewhere else." My mother had insisted. "My hotel and my front doorstep are not a boxing ring."

"I'm very sorry Mrs. Gethin." Ralphie had immediately replied apologetically. "He just flew at me, I couldn't stop him."

"That's because you Ralphie jumped into bed with my missus." The man had explained.

"I didn't know you two were that serious." Ralphie had confessed as he had quickly attempted to justify his actions. "I just went to see her and one thing led to another. I thought you might be just like a ship passing in the night."

"No Ralphie that is the woman that I am

going to marry." The man had swiftly replied. "Whereas you Ralphie, you are the ship that passes in the night and that moors yourself in other men's harbors."

"Okay Ralphie, you need to come to a gentleman's agreement." My mother had advised. "You have to agree that in future, you'll stay away from his wife to be and leave her alone."

"Okay Mrs. Gethin, I'll do that." Ralphie had immediately agreed.

"Do you agree to the truce?" My mother had asked as she had turned to face the other man.

"Yes, but if he breaks that agreement, I'll knock his dam lights out." The man had threatened. "Consider today a warning call Ralphie and I don't warn people twice."

Approximately fifteen minutes later, once the man had calmed down and had totally vacated the area, we had congregated inside the lounge and as my mother had turned to face Ralphie, she had shaken her head at him to clearly communicate her disapproval with regards to his actions. Just a few minutes later I had been sent to bed and as I'd left the lounge and then had walked along the hallway quite slowly, I had overheard my mother as she had given Ralphie a stiff warning about the women that he chose to associate with.

"You've really got to be more careful Ralphie because he knew exactly where to find you." My mother had warned. "You can't live your life jumping in and out of another man's bed because one day one of them will stick a pillow down your throat."

"I know Mrs. Gethin, I know." Ralphie had agreed. "I'll try to be more careful in future, it won't happen again."

"Make sure it doesn't Ralphie because I can't have fist fights on my doorstep every time you stay here." My mother had insisted. "A little bit of fun can cause a lot of heartbreak, remember that."

Once I had entered inside my room and had lain down to rest, I'd thoughtfully begun to consider Ralphie's evening of mayhem and drama and although I had been partially quite scared by the man's anger, I'd also almost admired Ralphie's bravery because he hadn't run away with his tail between his legs and so he had to some extent, taken full responsibility for his mischievous actions. However, that night had taught me a hugely valuable lesson when it came to the issue of men and the women that they loved and that had simply been that some men would fight to the death for the women that they loved and no matter how much Ralphie had charmed people, charm hadn't been enough or able to save him from a tidal wave of anger, regardless of whether his boat had already sailed or had remained moored to that particular dock of passion.

One of the funniest incidents however, that had occurred during the time of my mother's ownership of the Happyvale Hotel and my teenage years had happened on the day that I often refer to as the Humpty Dumpty Hump Day which had occurred one Saturday afternoon when two tourists had spent the entire afternoon locked inside one of the bathrooms upstairs. Apparently, the two lovers had initially entered into the bathroom together for a bit of passionate excitement but somehow, since the male lover in this instance had been very overweight and had tried to slip into a very complex, awkward sexual position, they had become stuck between the toilet and the actual bath mid-passion and so they had been unable to leave the room, or their passionate embrace for hours and hours.

Due to the couple's naked state, passionate entanglement and potential embarrassment, they had not raised the alarm for several hours as they had struggled to free themselves but eventually, they'd had to surrender due to hungry stomachs and had called out for assistance. Since it had been a Saturday afternoon, most of the guests that had usually occupied the guest rooms on the third floor had been out and about but fortunately for the two, one of the female Resies called Maria had finally returned from a trip to the local shops and she had heard their muffled cries and pleas for help as she'd sauntered past the bathroom en-route to her guest room.

In a matter of just minutes Maria had not only discovered the two lover's predicament but she had also managed to establish that they had been stuck inside the bathroom for several hours and so she'd of course immediately rushed back downstairs to my mother's door which she had then knocked very loudly upon. Due to all the commotion and being that I had naturally been a curious sort of chap in my teenage years, I had sauntered out into the main ground floor hotel hallway to satisfy my curiosity where I had found a disturbed Maria in the midst of a deep conversation about the matter with my mother.

"They're stuck inside the bathroom Mrs. Gethin." Maria had explained. "And apparently, they've been trapped in there for hours."

"Don't worry Maria, I'll sort it out." My mother had immediately reassured her as she had quickly plucked a set of keys from the hook by the door and then stepped out into the hallway. "I'll have them out of there in a jiffy."

Just a few seconds later my mother had rushed up the stairs towards the third-floor bathroom and so I had naturally started to follow her, partially to satisfy my own curiosity and partially to see if I could possibly be of any kind of assistance. Quite unfortunately however, once my mother had arrived on the third floor she had rapidly discovered that this particular problem could not be solved by her alone since the lock on the bathroom door had been internal and absolutely inaccessible from her position and as I had watched, a quick frustrated shake of her head had clearly illustrated her absolute frustration to me.

One possible option had existed which had been to kick the entire door down but as I had realized at the time, my physical build hadn't really been suitable or adult enough for such boisterous activities and so that meant, my potential to assist had really been rather limited. In terms of my build and structure, I hadn't been a muscular kind of chap and I'd even verged upon what one classify as slightly skinny and so I had felt absolutely certain that the destruction of a locked bathroom door had been a physical challenge that had lain just outside the scope of my physical prowess.

Since the two guests had not been locked inside a guest room at the time, there had been no actual spare key that my mother had access to and so the situation had really been quite complicated and had seemed almost impossible to resolve on the spot. Although a few of the male hotel guests had been far more muscular than myself and even what one might consider physically powerful, none of those guests had been around at the time and so in the end, my mother had, had to call the actual fire brigade in to get the two lovers out.

After the fire brigade had arrived and they had dealt with the locked door via a heavy chunk of metal which they'd utilized to bang it open, the two lovers that had been stuck inside the bathroom had then quickly been offered bathrobes by my mother which I had already been sent to collect from her room downstairs. Due to the two lover's nakedness and the very awkward situation, some very sheepish and apologetic expressions had adorned their faces as they had thanked the fire brigade and then the three fire fighters had vacated the premises. Once my mother had given the bathroom a quick inspection, she had then returned to the hall where she had faced the two lovers with a semi amused expression upon her face as she'd begun to address them about the incident.

"Bathrooms can be very slippery places you know." My mother had advised the two as she had shaken her head. "It's probably best to stick to bedrooms in future."

"Yes Mrs. Gethin." The male guest had replied.

Fortunately for the two guests who had both been short term visitors at the hotel, there hadn't been many people around at the time to be an actual audience to their awkward predicament and so the incident had been less of an embarrassment for them but if it had occurred on a Saturday night as I'd been fully aware, they'd have been the laughing stock of the whole hotel. Since it had been early evening by the time the two had finally been rescued from the bathroom, once a few more words of wisdom and advice had been given to the two lovers, my mother had then led me back downstairs in order to prepare our usual evening family meal but as we'd walked, she had warned me about the dangers that I may face, if I chose to dabble excessively in the deep waves of desire, the rampant tides of sensual lust and if I swam too frequently in the stormy seas of passion.

"You see Steven how people can get caught up in trouble when they jump into mischief." My mother had warned. "You have to be careful where you lay your head in life because not all pillows are made from feathers and not all beds are comfortable to lie in because some are made from very hard, jagged, sharp rocks."

Over the years my mother had given me many chunks of wise advice and although I hadn't always fully appreciated her arms of wisdom and her hands of experience as I had grown older, I'd learnt that her observations about life, the world and the people that occupied it had been spot on. Due to the hotel's location and my mother's situation, she had learnt a lot about people as she had weathered the storms of life and had trudged through the valleys of hardship, equipped with nothing but hard work and sheer determination and somehow, she had always managed to keep her head held up high, despite the many difficulties and hard times that she'd faced. In fact, at times even now, I often reflect upon my mother's wise words and wish that I had listened to each one much more carefully because she really had experienced life and she had seen not only the best in people but also the absolute worst and although that day, her words had been coated in amusement, purely due to the situation, her message to me had still been very serious, totally sincere and profoundly true as I'd discovered later in life.

Strange days and nights had really been quite common at the hotel, especially on the sardine packed weekends when the human overflow had spilled out onto the stairs and into the halls of the building and one such night that I have never been able to forget, I often refer to as the night of Sardines in Passion. Much like a usual weekend night, the stairs and halls had been jam packed with human bodies but on this particular night, even more so because apparently, there had been some kind of popular event in the nearby high street and so afterwards, people had flocked to any kind of accommodation that they had been able to find, predominantly in a drunken or drug happy state to grab a few hours rest.

Quite naturally, since the Happyvale Hotel had been just a stone's throw away from the bottom end of the high street and within easy financial reach, many had flocked to my mother's hotel that Saturday night and had accepted whatever space had been available as usual. Although at times I had felt quite sympathetic towards the human bodies that had been packed into the halls and stairs on those weekends of chaotic occupation, my mother had never seemed to be bothered by it and she had simply explained to me that the hotel's four walls had been far safer to sleep in than the streets.

In those days transport facilities during the nightly hours had been really quite limited and the usually drunken revelers had predominantly, journeyed to Camden for a night out which had normally been jam packed with outlandish activities and as much alcohol and drugs as they had been able to lay their hands on. Usually, by the time those guests had arrived at the hotel, they had steeped their human bodies in as much alcohol, drugs, flirtation and mayhem as they'd been able to fit in to any given weekend night and quite often, it had seemed as if their only intention had simply been to party until they physically dropped from sheer exhaustion and so my mother had accommodated them for a fraction of the price, if they had accepted a spot on the floor.

"The floors inside the hotel are far safer than spending a night out in the streets." My mother had always said. "And in that state, you never know what might happen to people out there."

For so many reasons and in so many ways, the packed in sardine weekend nights had suited both parties, the drunken, stoned revelers and my mother and so as far back as I can remember, such nights had been a regular weekend occurrence. The tenner or a fiver required to bed down on the floor for the night, or even just for a few hours had been a preferable alternative for many as opposed to the huge cab fares that might have been incurred to transport them back to their homes. Due to the potential safety that the hotel's walls had offered to the revelers and the greatly reduced risk of any drunken mishaps, the sardine nights had been considered by many a preferred option and although it hadn't been completely without any risks at all, my mother had always tried to ensure that she had kept males and females quite separate and had often placed them at opposite ends of any vacant spaces.

Although that particular Saturday night had initially started out in quite an organized fashion as my mother had packed some people into the halls and stairs and even allowed some people to occupy the lounge, she had tried to instill and maintain some kind of rotation system that had allowed people at least four hours sleep before they had been moved along. Due to the drunken state of the guests however, all kinds of shenanigans had followed and on one of my trips to the bathroom since I had woken up because of the noise, I'd almost fallen over a drunken couple involved in a very intimate embrace. However, my exposure to drunken human antics that night had not ended there because once I had managed to make my way through the sea of bodies on the floor, most of whom had been asleep at the time, much to my surprise, when

I'd finally arrived at the bathroom door and then stepped inside the bathroom, I had found two people inside it engaged in some very intimate sexual acts.

Part of me had frozen as I had simply stared at the two and then watched them for a few minutes, since I'd been slightly curious about their sexual activities and had just stumbled into puberty and hence my body had quite naturally been stirred, aroused and awakened. However, just a minute or two later, my mother had ventured out into the hallway and she had spotted the open bathroom door and so she had then quickly rushed towards it and retrieved me from the doorway as she had attempted to rush me back towards my own room and back to my bed.

Despite all my mother's efforts however, that hadn't quite been the end of my night because although I had returned to my room, I'd still needed to use the bathroom and so I had waited for a little while, until I'd felt that my mother might have settled down for the night and then I had bravely prepared to venture out of my room again. A hopeful wish had lain inside my mind as I had opened the door of my room and then crept out into the hallway that the occupants of the bathroom might have finished their sexual entanglement by that point because to be perfectly frank, I'd really needed to urinate and as I had been fully aware at that the time, not even a sensual arousal could delay that bodily requirement indefinitely.

Unfortunately, and much to my total dismay, I had rapidly discovered that even though the couple I'd walked in on had finished their passionate entanglement by that point in time, the same bathroom had it seemed then been occupied by another couple in search of passion, irrespective of the fact that my body had been in absolute dire need of an urgent urinary release. Since there had been bathrooms on each floor of the hotel, I had started to pick my way through the human bodies asleep on the floor and then had begun to make my upstairs but as I'd arrived upon the first floor, I had found the bathroom locked and several moans and groans had emanated from behind the door which had clearly indicated that the second bathroom had not been an option for me either. Once I had visited the bathrooms on every floor which had all been occupied by passion seekers, I'd then begun to make my way back downstairs but I had absolutely no clue what to do really because there had appeared to be no solution to my need to urinate but as I'd arrived back on the ground floor, I had finally decided to try the back garden and so had then begun to make my way towards the back door.

A small rock had been found on the ground next to the door and then lodged and wedged into a corner of the back doorway as I begun to make my way outside, just to ensure that I would be able to get back inside the building once I'd relieved myself as I had retained the hope that I might be able to urinate somewhere outside the actual hotel itself. Just a few minutes later I had found a quiet spot close to the shed and so I had turned to face away from the building and then had rapidly relieved myself as a huge sigh of relief had escaped from my lips. Once my bodily functions had been well and truly attended to, I had then started to make my way back towards the back door but much to my absolute horror, as I'd arrived beside it I had quickly discovered that the small rock had been dislodged and that the back door had not only been shut but also that it had been actually locked.

For approximately the next twenty minutes I had knocked upon the back door in the hope that someone might be close to the door, hear the knocks and then open it but no one had appeared to be nearby, or no one close to the door it seemed had been in an awakened state. Due to the chilliness of the air, I had finally decided to retreat and seek shelter inside the shed in order to consider my options because there had been no way out of the back garden that led directly to the front street since the buildings next to the hotel had all been joined together which had meant, I'd have to jump over a few walls and fences to reach the end of street and then walk all the way around the buildings to arrive at the front door where I'd have to knock upon the front door and then face my mother. Explanations as I had already known, would definitely be demanded by my mother and a likely outcome of those actions and explanations would be bread and butter for dinner for a week and so

I'd felt quite reluctant to pursue that option but as I had sat for a couple of hours in the drafty, cold shed that option had gradually become more and more attractive to me.

Finally, I had decided to brave any potential punishments as I'd left the shed and then begun to make my way towards the wall that separated the back garden from the garden next door. Once I had arrived next to the wall, I'd then begun to enthusiastically tackle it as I had attempted to climb over it however, in the midst of my attempts, somehow, I'd managed to catch my foot on a piece of washing line wire that had been hidden amongst the weeds and so I had quickly fallen back down to the ground and twisted my ankle. For the next couple of hours, I had just sat upon the ground, unable to get up and walk anywhere and unable to help myself but fortunately, once the early Sunday morning hours had arrived, so too had help as one of the guests had suddenly opened up the back door, stepped outside and then discovered my situation.

Once the hotel guest who had been one of the long-term Resies called Patrick had arrived beside me, he had quickly offered me a hand of support which I had immediately accepted and then he'd even helped me walk back towards the back door but as we had entered back inside the building, I'd pleaded with him not to say a word to my mother. A deep seeded worry had occupied and lain inside my mind that if my wander outside the building in the middle of the night had been discovered, I'd have definitely been punished and be given nothing but bread and butter for dinner for a week and that hadn't been something that I had wanted to experience along with my injuries which as I'd known at the time, would probably remain with my physical body for at least a week.

"Don't worry Steven, I won't say a word." Patrick had promised. "I was young once too you know, so I know what it's like when you really need to pee and there's nowhere to do it."

"Thanks." I had replied.

True to Patrick's word, he had not uttered a single word to my mother that day or any other day and I had just been so grateful that it had been Patrick that had discovered my predicament as opposed to Snide Stuart or Fishy Frank. Unlike some of my enemies who had jumped on any opportunity that they could possibly find to get me in trouble with my mother, Patrick had not utilized my misfortunate accident against me and so my secret had remained intact and unspoken and as far as my mother had been concerned, I had just sprained my ankle on a rock in the garden when I'd gone outside for some fresh air that morning.

Much to my total dismay and utter heartbreak, one day my mother's reign over the Happyvale Hotel had finally come to an end but her departure from the hotel and life itself had left behind many happy memories of the times that we had experienced, lived and shared together up until that point in time. Although my mother's physical form had no longer walked through life beside me after her departure, the fond memories that we had shared, many of which still clung to the walls of the building that we had called our family home for so many years, have always remained with me and those treasured memories still live inside my heart until this very day.

The Happyvale Hotel had never quite managed to stumble up the star ranks into the top tiers of hotel royalty and it had never become the lavish, luxury establishment that at one time my mother had perhaps hoped that it might be but it had kept our family financially on our feet and its walls had provided enough resources to enable my mother's children to clamber through life and arrive at adulthood in one piece. For me, the achievements that my mother had achieved through hard work, sheer determination and courageous guts, despite her solitary status and her lack of support from the outside world, have always remained with me until this day and I now truly recognize and appreciate, how truly hard she'd worked, how much she had struggled to give her children all that she could, how much she'd had to cope with and endure and how much she had sacrificed just to ensure that our childhoods had been stable and decent.

TIME TO STEP UP

After my mother had passed away, the responsibility of the hotel had fallen straight into my lap but to be perfectly honest, it hadn't been one that I had been quite ready or prepared for and in some respects, it hadn't even been something that I'd particularly wanted. Technically, although I had spent my entire childhood and my teenage years life inside the Happyvale Hotel, I'd never actually been involved in its actual maintenance or the administration that its quasi corporate existence had required and so for me, it had been a very reluctant, sudden dive into the deep end of hotel management as I had assumed what I'd considered at the time to be a very heavy responsibility.

Deep down inside, I had felt quite emotionally bound to the commercial premises by all the hard work that my mother had put into the hotel for the many years of her life that she had dedicated to it and so in many ways, I'd really wanted to honor her memory in a meaningful manner. A deep seeded commitment and loyalty had definitely existed on my mother's part that had tied our family to a building that had essentially kept us clothed and fed throughout my childhood and teenage years but as I had rapidly discovered, the wish to live up to a noble desire certainly hadn't been as easy to live with as it had been to dream or romanticize about and that reality had struck me very hard, extremely quickly. Suddenly however, a very heavy duty had fallen straight onto my quite slight shoulders and although I had definitely not been prepared for it and hadn't particularly wanted it, I'd attempted to carry the load in the hope that things would perhaps turn out as my mother had hoped and as she would have wanted them to.

Since the majority of my adult life up until that point had predominantly been quite corrupt because I had worked for years as a tout for some of the sleaziest strip bars in London where prostitution had been rife, hotel management had never really been something that I'd ever considered before as an actual career choice. Despite my lack of prior interest and experience however, I had tried to adapt irrespective of my very obvious shortcomings as I'd attempted to step up to the responsibility of the hotel and all the duties that such a responsibility had actually entailed. Sadly, and unfortunately however, as I had rapidly discovered within just the first few weeks of hotel ownership, noble intentions hadn't been able to provide a lifeline to absolute ignorance and that had been the first lesson that I'd learnt very quickly indeed because I had truly been way out of my depth and quite unable to reach any shores of meaningful recovery, or any banks of acceptable redemption.

Hotel guests had always come and gone throughout the course of my mother's life but when I had become the owner and manager of the hotel, I'd then actually had to pay far more attention to who had stayed, who'd left and who had actually been due to arrive. Some guests had stayed at the hotel for years and years when my mother had been alive and they had been private clients that had paid for their own accommodation themselves but when I had taken over the hotel that customer dynamic had suddenly changed because I'd been unable to cope with the financial fluctuations that had occurred.

A swarm of financial difficulties had suddenly zoomed into and swamped my life due to the empty, vacant rooms and those monetary responsibilities had almost completely drowned me as the economic realities of hotel ownership had flooded through and saturated almost every second of my life. Due to the heaviness of the responsibilities involved, I had consulted a few people that I'd known at the time and several people had advised me to accept government clients in need of temporary accommodation which at the time had seemed like the perfect solution. The main hope as I had fully embraced and embarked upon that course of action had been that some kind of financial stability would subsequently follow and I'd also felt at the time that through the provision of temporary accommodation, in some small way, the hotel would perhaps serve a useful purpose to the community around it and perhaps even reduce some of the housing problems in the area.

Despite all my noble and good intentions however, the hotel that my mother had bequeathed to me had then quickly turned into a dumping ground for anyone and everyone that had wanted to fill it with human bodies and due to my lack of experience, knowledge and skills, I had been absolutely powerless to stop it. The provision of accommodation to government clients had initially appealed to me for several reasons but the main positive factor had been deemed to be the financial stability that such a solution had seemed to offer because it had guaranteed and honored not only a basic rate for each room occupied but also consistent payments from the local authority. Since it had been agreed that the majority of the hotel's rooms would fall under that agreement that had also meant that most of the guest rooms would be occupied most of the time and so, the provision of temporary housing had seemed to offer potential solutions to me that would resolve at least two huge issues of concern.

Prior to the acceptance of government clients, I had worried profusely about vacant rooms and occupancy rates because the responsibility to fill up the hotel's empty guest rooms had lain at my feet but I'd been reassured that quite often government clients stayed in temporary accommodation for a few months at a time and so I had initially felt as if a huge weight had been lifted from my shoulders. According to what I had been told at the time by trusted associates and sources, most of the clients would stay in the hotel for longer time periods than just a week or a fortnight and so that would at least guarantee a degree of occupancy for a fixed time period that could perhaps even last for several months per client although I had also been told that some people actually stayed in temporary accommodation for far longer than just a few months.

In theory, the consistency that such agreements seemed to offer had definitely appealed to me at that time because there had appeared to be an element of certainty that could actually be relied upon which I had felt, would definitely be beneficial to all the parties involved and so, when I'd had the chance to make an agreement of that kind, I had literally jumped at the opportunity to do so. However, as I had rapidly discovered, once I'd begun to participate, due to all the bureaucracy that had accompanied such arrangements and the reduced payments, those kind of accommodation provisions had other disadvantages and other kinds of challenges attached to them, all of which I had initially been totally ignorant about.

Due to my lack of experience when it had come to the actual issue of hotel management, some of the guests that had occupied the hotel's guest rooms had presented me with tons of issues and mountains of trouble and so I had rapidly discovered that the problematic issues had not just revolved around guest occupancy rates, bureaucracy or even the reliability of payments and unfortunately, had even involved some of the guests themselves. In fact, as I now reflect back upon the very early days of my hotel ownership I actually realize that some people had taken full advantage of my lacking because they had made the most of my failures and capitalized upon each one and at the time, since I had been quite overwhelmed due to all the heavy responsibilities and had felt almost buried by the mass of problems that I'd faced, I had been quite unable to stand up to them effectively.

Despite the fact that I had been totally out of my depth in every way imaginable however, that had not managed to dissuade me from my attempts to honor my mother's memory and nor had it reduced my desire to keep the Happyvale Hotel's doors open. A deep seeded desire had formed, grown and existed inside my mind and heart that had wanted to keep the Happyvale Hotel under my family's ownership, since my mother had devoted so much of her life to it and so, I had continued to soldier on just as I'd seen my own mother do for so many years before her departure from life. Some stiff glasses of whiskey and bottles of wine had rapidly become my regular companions and my best friends, purely due to the stress levels that I'd had to face which had suddenly, increased very dramatically as I had tried to handle the challenges that hotel ownership and the hospitality industry had presented to me and had tried to wade through the huge responsibilities that hotel management had demanded from every second of my life.

New guests had flowed through the hotel's doors and hallways as often as the wine had flowed down the back of my throat in those early days and some of them had literally shocked the hell out of me as I had struggled to step up to not only my mother's wishes but also to my new life as a hotel owner. Very sadly however, I had quickly learnt that my saunter down the lane of supposed grandeur into what had initially seemed like a potential oasis of prosperity had been nothing more than a wade into a very murky, deep swamp of heavy, stressful responsibilities and as I'd stumbled deeper and deeper into that swamp, it had almost seemed as if it had wanted to drag me down into its stressful depths and then consume me.

When it came to the actual name of the hotel which I had also inherited, Happyvale Hotel had always given the impression and evoked the assumption of joy, laughter and pleasant accommodation however, the hotel under my ownership had not only challenged that name but had also been situated a million miles away from it because it had been far from a pleasant place to stay. Due to the lack of interest in the hotel and the lack of respect for the premises shown by many of the hotel's guests, once I had assumed ownership minor emergencies had arisen almost every single day and major emergencies had been a frequent occurrence because some of the residents that I'd welcomed into the building had it seemed, absolutely no respect at all for the property that they had been invited to occupy and to live inside.

Unlike my mother's period of ownership which had been reasonably orderly, except on some chaotic weekend nights and in most respects, quite well controlled, my period of ownership had been a chaotic mess from start to finish and throughout those early days, it had been like a flurry of drama every single day. In fact, as I reflect back, I remember that the early days of my hotel ownership had been a total disaster in every way that each day possibly could have been but a deep desire had still lain inside my heart to be the son that my mother had wanted me to be and to achieve the things that she would have been proud of and so, I had persevered.

One of my first baptism's into total chaos and the first huge, major emergency that I had faced had occurred within the first couple of months after I had not only assumed control and ownership of the hotel but I had also already started to accept clients in need of accommodation from the local authority. Since it had been such a huge incident and it had gone above and beyond the usual chaos and daily drama that had usually occupied the hotel's interior along with the guests, it had left had a huge imprint upon my mind because it had been my first real crisis situation and so I have never been able to forget about the flood which had occurred late one night without any warning at all.

According to my usual daily evening routine I had eaten dinner at around seven which had on this occasion consisted of an actual steak that one of the guests had brought back from work for me which I had also consumed with my usual bottle of red wine. Since one of the guests at that time had worked for one of the luxury food stores situated in the city center they had brought a steak back from work that day especially for me and in fact that had been one of the few perks of my hotel ownership in that a few of the private clients had at times had given me gifts of appreciation for being tolerant, empathetic or lenient towards them in some capacity, whenever they had faced various difficulties in life. Once I had eaten my evening meal and once I'd conducted my usual nightly checks of the building which had usually occurred at around nine each night I had then returned to my living room and bedroom area to relax however, just one hour or so after my return as I'd begun to prepare for a peaceful, decent night's sleep, quite suddenly I had heard some yells that had emanated from one of the upper floors.

Since the hotel had been split across five floors with three guests' rooms and a communal bathroom on each floor inclusive of the ground floor where there had also been not only a communal bathroom but also a small communal kitchen area that adjoined a general guest lounge, it had initially been impossible for me to know exactly which floor the yells had originated from without closer inspection. Due to the nature of the yells which had sounded very urgent, I had quickly abandoned my lounge and then had started to make my way towards the source of the noise and towards the hotel staircase. On my way up the stairs however, much to my surprise, I had almost bumped into an alarmed guest called Paul who had been a quiet, well-mannered man in his early fifties and he had then rapidly begun to explain to me the reason for all the commotion.

"Mr. Gethin, there's water gushing all over the place, it's like a flood." Paul had gasped. "And it's even coming through the ceilings. What about the lights, it could be dangerous?"

"Where's all the water coming from Paul?" I had asked.

"I think it's coming from one of the bathrooms upstairs." Paul had replied. "Probably the one on the top floor."

Every word that had been spoken by Paul

had seeped in fear, panic and alarm and once I had listened to him to speak for a few seconds, I'd then allowed him to lead the way towards the source of the flood as I had continued to ask him some more questions, most of which he had possessed none of the actual answers to. Just a few minutes later and much to my absolute horror, as we had both arrived on the top floor I had almost gasped in total shock as I'd started wade my way along the hall towards the bathroom at the other end of it because the water had been almost halfway up my calf and a guest had it transpired, let the water run for hours and left an actual plug in the actual plughole of the bath itself. Unfortunately, to my total dismay, the flood had it seemed not only affected the top floor of the hotel however, because by that point some of the water had reached the stairs and had begun a downward descent and some of it had even managed to seep through the floorboards and into the electrical system which had also meant, a real danger had definitely existed.

“I need to switch of all the lights inside the building immediately.” I had rapidly concluded. "You're absolutely right Paul, this is definitely, very dangerous."

In a matter of just seconds I had stepped inside the actual bathroom, approached the taps and then I'd quickly turned each one off and removed the plug from the actual bath after which point I had then hurriedly waded my way back towards the bathroom door. Despite all the commotion, the culprit and offender that had left the bathroom in such a state had been nowhere to be seen and as the water had started to slowly subside, I had then rushed back down the stairs and as I'd made my way through the halls, I had attempted to turn off all the lights that I'd been able to access immediately.

Once I had arrived back on the ground floor, I'd then accessed the mains and I had quickly turned off all the electricity and lights via the fuse box as an additional safety measure before I'd collected some torches and then rapidly returned to the top floor of the building and the flooded bathroom with a bucket, some towels and a few cloths inside my hands. Due to all the commotion I had also had to provide brief explanations en-route to some of the other guests as to why all the lights had been switched off and I'd even handed out a couple of torches to them on my way back up to the fifth floor so that they would have some kind of visibility in the darkness that by that point had already blanketed the interior of the building.

For approximately the next thirty minutes I had done nothing else but scoop up water and much to my surprise, Paul had actually started to assist me, even though it had not been his actual responsibility to do so. Inside my mind as I had worked however, a few suspicions had definitely, silently lurked and lingered as to who had actually been responsible for the flood in the first place but no one had appeared on the fifth-floor landing since I'd arrived there besides Paul and myself and so, it had been hard to put a finger on the actual culprit. A mop had been found in the nearby cleaning cupboard and as I had continued to tackle the mess, Paul had very graciously, decided to stick around and had even assisted me.

Once all the water had been wiped and mopped up and once the bathroom had been restored to a reasonable degree of functionality that had been somewhat satisfactory, I had then thanked Paul and made my way back downstairs. Truthfully however, I had felt absolutely livid at the time because the mess had taken a good couple of hours to clean up and the person responsible for it had obviously not bothered to take ownership for that mess or even offered to assist in any capacity, another issue which had bothered and irritated me profusely.

After all the palaver had died down, some explanations had been provided to some curious guests that had gathered in the ground floor hallway and once the power had been switched back on, I had then finally returned to the sanctuary of my own room to find a remnant of peace from that day's chaos which had been a definite storm that had rocked my boat of life. Inside my mind as I had prepared to rest that night however, I'd continued to ponder over the issue of who had actually been responsible for the actual flood itself in the first place but I had been none the wiser and that strange mystery has in fact, remained with me until this very day.

The next very strange, large emergency that had occurred had happened just a few months after I had taken over ownership of the hotel and it had shocked and alarmed me even more than the first but initially, it hadn't actually seemed as significant or as chaotic. Unlike the first huge emergency however, the second huge incident had actually related to a guest called Vince, who had one day, rather strangely, suddenly, totally vanished without a trace or any kind of explanation. Initially, Vince had seemed no different from any of the other guests in many respects but after he had stayed at the hotel for a couple of weeks, I had started to notice that he had been quite withdrawn, rather quiet and slightly timid and that he'd always seemed to be preoccupied by a continuous stream of worries which had decorated his forehead with multiple lines of stress that had been engraved into his face.

Due to the agreements that I had made with the local authority every single one of their clients had to sign a register each night and every morning to confirm that they had occupied a guest room and been on the premises for the entire night and Vince had been no exception to that general rule. The guest register had to be checked by myself twice a day and so I had checked it religiously every morning and each night to ensure that their clients had been on the premises and that they had utilized their guest rooms and since Vince had been one of their clients, I'd had an actual responsibility to monitor his occupancy. Prior to that point in time Vince had very consistently signed the register every single morning and each night as per the local authority's requirements had stipulated and so there had been no issues at all as far as I had been concerned about his occupancy of a guest room inside the hotel but when his name had suddenly, disappeared from the register, I had instantly been quite concerned about his absence because it had seemed totally out of character for him and highly unusual.

On the whole, unlike some of the other far louder, more rambunctious guests, Vince had been a well-mannered man in his fifties with peppered grey hair and I had quickly grown accustomed to his quiet but worried persona which since his arrival had definitely been greatly preferred to some of the more troublesome guests. Truthfully however, I hadn't really spent that much time with him since he had initially arrived because I'd usually only seen him a few times a week and never for more than a few minutes on each occasion.

Once two days had gone by without the appearance of Vince's name on the local authority client register and there had been absolutely no sight of Vince by myself, I had then raised the alarm and notified the local authority due to my own worries and in accordance with our stipulated agreements. In response to my alert the local authority had simply advised me to keep his guest room reserved for him for the next fortnight in case he returned and since they had agreed to meet the cost, I had immediately complied willingly with their instructions and had continued to wait for his return.

Some of the private clients that had stayed at the hotel had gone to and fro as they had wished too and so it really hadn't been that unusual for me not to see a guest every single day, or even at times for a few days and as long as they'd paid for their accommodation in advance, their rooms had always been kept for them and reserved solely for their occupancy. However, the situation with Vince had been slightly different due to the fact that he had been a local authority client and so he'd been expected to sign the guest register twice a day to verify his presence on the premises and his room occupancy each night.

Rather curiously, after a whole week had gone by, there had still been absolutely no signs of Vince and so his continued, prolonged absence had really started to worry me and as a result, I had grown far more alarmed and so on the final day of his absence which had been a Thursday, I had decided to investigate his disappearance myself. The whole building and grounds I had decided had to be checked and I'd also decided to ask the other guests when they had last seen Vince to see if anyone else could shed any light upon his strange disappearance. Since Ursula usually had a lot more contact with the guests each day than myself, purely because she had been responsible for cleaning the communal areas of the building, she had naturally been my first port of call as I had eagerly sought her out and then had encouraged her to join my search for Vince.

According to hotel's agreed weekly cleaning routine, Ursula had even given some of the guest rooms a once over with a hoover and a light dust once a week, if the guest that had occupied a guest room had wanted her to do so which had meant, she had spent more time inside the hotel's guest rooms than I had ever done. Quite strangely however, according to Ursula, Vince had never once asked her for that service and he had never once that she had seen, allowed anyone else into his guest room besides himself and since neither of us had ever seen Vince with any visitors that had meant that there had been no one else besides the other guests to discuss his actual disappearance with.

Naturally, the first place that I had looked for Vince and had searched for any clues with Ursula in tow had been Vince's actual guest room which I had been able to access quite easily because I had kept a set of spare keys to all the hotel rooms in my office inside a small security case, just in case any emergencies ever arose. The loss of room keys had been a regular occurrence at the hotel and so the small, glass security case and the keys it had contained had ensured that if I had to, I could quite easily cut another key for a guest, or even access a guest room myself in an absolute emergency. Usually however, I had never entered into a guest's room without their prior permission, knowledge and consent simply out of respect for other people's privacy and I'd pretty much left the guests to their own devices unless there had been an emergency situation that had required urgent intervention from myself.

Quite eerily however, once I had stepped inside Vince's room along with Ursula, I'd found it really quite empty and not many personal belongings had actually been present which had struck me as slightly strange at the time, since Vince had been a local authority client. The local authority guests as I had been very much aware had usually packed as much as they possibly could into their rooms since they had been in-between permanent homes because they usually, had lots of possessions that they'd wished to move homes with but Vince's room had looked almost bare and so I'd immediately noticed that emptiness because it really had been very unusual. Initially, when Vince had first arrived at the hotel, I had noticed that he had brought with him just a small suitcase of belongings and from what I'd been able to see from the emptiness of his room, apparently that small case of items really had been all that he'd had.

True to Ursula's usual stringent form and very hygienic nature, not long after we had entered inside Vince's room, it had been given a quick once over with a hoover, the windows had been opened up and the surfaces had then been given a light dust, since the interior of the room had smelt, really quite musty. Neither of us had seen Vince for at least a week and the fact that his room had smelt a bit musty, had rapidly clarified and confirmed to us both that he had probably not visited it in that time period in any capacity at all.

For the next few hours of that day, once Vince's room had been given a light clean and inspected for any clues to his whereabouts,

Ursula and I had walked through the entire interior of the building and we had knocked up every single guest room door and I'd questioned all the other guests about their last sighting of Vince. No one however, had seen Vince for the past week and as I had begun to process each guest's last account and their most recent memories of Vince, I'd started to feel the anxiety build up silently inside of me like a wall of tense worry but this wall had been absolutely impenetrable and it had not allowed my mind to climb or jump over it in order to find a place of rest, or any peace. Throughout that day a number of questions had flooded through my mind and the visit to Vince's room had provided me with absolutely none of the answers such as, had he left the building, when had he left the hotel and where had he last gone and unfortunately, none of the other guests had been able to shed any light upon any of those mysterious questions either.

Some dark thoughts had begun to occupy the forefront of my mind and it had almost felt as if each one had built a campsite in amongst my thoughts as I had continued the search along with Ursula and we had stepped out of the back door into the back garden as the evening had stepped into the heart of the city. Since Vince's absence had seemed so highly unusual at the time and absolutely no clues had appeared to provide an indication of his actual whereabouts, I had been unable to rest my mind throughout that entire day and so the evening's entrance had simply, silently greeted my worried mind which had still remained without any actual answers. A deep concern had definitely lingered inside my human frame as I had started to lead Ursula around the back garden and had then begun to inspect every inch of it as I'd searched high and low for any kind of clues before I had finally headed towards the quite rickety, worse for wear, wooden shed at the bottom of the garden.

"What shall we do if we don't find him Mr. Gethin?" Ursula had asked.

"I'm not totally sure yet Ursula, let's just see if we can find him first." I had replied as I'd approached the shed. "I'm sure he's absolutely fine, he probably just went to visit some friends or something."

Strangely enough, throughout that day as

we had searched, I hadn't even actually considered what might happen if I hadn't managed to find Vince or some traces of his whereabouts by the end of that day and really and truly, I had absolutely no desire to find out because his disappearance by that point, had started to worry me profusely. My main concern throughout that entire day had simply revolved around Vince's absence and so I hadn't even considered for a second what I would do, if we hadn't managed to find any sign of him by the time our search ended and even though I had reassured Ursula to some extent that we would find him, deep down inside myself, I'd remained totally unconvinced that Vince would indeed, actually be found.

My usual attempts at paperwork or any other administrative tasks had that day, been totally abandoned as I had made Vince and his whereabouts my top priority and as I'd focused solely upon my task. Although usually, it would have been a very pleasant change to get away from the usual paperwork for a day, due to the unpleasant nature of the distraction, the day had not lightened my mood in any way and if anything, my mood had been far damper than usual. A nervous air of uncertainty had definitely reigned over my mind that day, practically all day and truthfully, I hadn't been entirely sure what should be done if I either couldn't find Vince or if we managed to find him and something very awful had indeed, actually happened to him.

Since the day had started to draw to a close the duskiness of the evening had already begun to settle in as I had arrived in front of the shed with Ursula in tow and although technically, Ursula should have actually left for home by that point in time, due to Vince's absence she had committed herself to the search and so, she had stayed far later than usual. Quite horrifyingly however, as I had reached for the handle of the shed door and then had started to pull it open a very strange stench had suddenly, instantly greeted and rapidly begun to infiltrate, penetrate and fill my nostrils and my stomach had almost retched as I'd started to process the awful possibility that the strange stench that I had been able to smell might in fact, actually be Vince. Nothing but nervous drops of sweat had dripped from my forehead like drops of anxiety as I had prepared myself for the worst and hoped for the best as a multitude of horrified questions had run silently through my mind like a torrential flood of shocked dismay because the smell certainly hadn't been pleasant and it had almost knocked me totally off balance.

Deep down inside my gut a horrible feeling had started to tie my stomach and airways up in fearful knots as I had prepared to look inside the actual interior of the shed and by that point, I had felt almost totally convinced by the foul stench that Vince lay inside its wooden interior. Nothing else outside the shed had shown any visible traces of Vince but that foul smell had definitely convinced me that something foul had definitely occurred and the likelihood had been that, that something foul had related to Vince's person. For a few seconds I had suddenly, stopped and paused as fearful hesitation had rapidly gripped every part of my mind and heart, before I'd finally turned to face Ursula and had then decisively taken her arm and had started to steer her away from the shed and the partially open shed door.

"I don't think you should stand so close to

the shed Ursula." I had advised.

"Okay, Mr. Gethin." Ursula had immediately agreed as she had quickly followed my lead and stepped back from the shed.

A very deep inhalation had been taken as I had left Ursula's side and I'd started to walk back towards the shed door as I had attempted to extract all the bravery that I'd been able to muster from inside my person and had begun to prepare myself for the actual moment of discovery. When I had conducted the premises checks each morning and every night, since I'd taken ownership of the hotel, I had rarely visited the shed in the back garden and so, I hadn't even seen its interior myself for quite a while but for the first time ever, I'd really feared what might actually be situated inside its quite flimsy, wooden plank walls. Deep down inside myself, I had definitely known as I'd walked back towards the shed that this moment of discovery would be absolutely traumatic and situated a million miles away from anything pleasant because the smell that had infiltrated and penetrated my nostrils had smelt so absolutely foul.

Vomit had seemed to line every inch of my interior as I had arrived back at the shed and had then pulled the door open wider and as I'd stepped inside the actual shed itself, the stench had flooded over me and had rapidly wrapped itself all around my human body in just a matter of seconds as I had started to tremble with absolute fear. In one corner of the shed I had immediately noticed a human body that had lain limp upon the ground, still and lifeless and all that I'd been able to hear as I had visually scanned the interior of the structure had been the buzz from the flies that had covered and found a home on that lifeless human frame as I'd peered into the depths of the shed and shuddered. For a few very unpleasant seconds I had been totally unable to move, speak or even breathe and it had almost felt as if I'd been glued to the spot as I had begun to silently process the horrible reality that Vince had definitely been found but that now, only his remains actually remained.

Due to my shock and confusion, a flurry of questions had suddenly begun to rapidly somersault through the passageways of my mind as I had started to question the events that might have led to Vince's death, such as how had Vince died, had someone else been responsible for his death and had that someone been a guest at the hotel that might even still be around. Nothing but silence had greeted me however, from Vince's lifeless form and that silence had only been broken by the buzz of the flies which had still continued to hover around his corpse.

Despite the many questions inside my mind however, I had remained completely still for another couple of minutes, unable to move and unable to utter a single word as I'd watched the insects crawl all over Vince's lifeless human remains in absolute horror and total shock. For the first time in my entire life that day, I had seen an actual human corpse in the process of decomposition which had absolutely horrified me and so I'd almost vomited as my stomach had retched repeatedly. No doubts at all had lain inside my mind however, as I had stood inside that shed with regards to Vince's actual life because by that point, it had definitely ended and his human body no longer even held a breath of life or a heartbeat of hope and so I had arrived, far too late to be of any help.

Just a few minutes later and once I had finally managed to shake myself out of my shocked paralysis, I'd then exited the shed but as I had begun to walk back towards Ursula, total shock and utter horror had remained inside my body as I'd continued to mentally process the sight and visual images of what I had just seen. Every step that I had taken as I'd crossed the garden and walked towards Ursula had been heavy because my body had felt weighed down by absolute trauma as I had prepared to break the terrible news to her and send her home for the day. Once I had arrived next to Ursula, I'd paused for a moment and had hesitated for a few seconds as I had stood directly in front of her and had just shaken my head as I'd attempted to dig deep within myself and find enough strength to utter a few verbal expressions to her because shock had continued to stifle not only my movements but also my tongue.

"Vince has passed away Ursula, I found him inside the shed." I had finally managed to blurt out and as each word had tumbled from my lips, I'd shaken my head in sadness. "You should go home and rest now, I'll sort things out from here." I had insisted. "And you can take the day off work tomorrow."

"Okay, Mr. Gethin." Ursula had replied as a few tears had started to trickle down her cheeks.

Every part of me had felt truly horrified as I had conveyed the sad, awful, tragic news to Ursula and due to the sudden shock, I had given her the next day of work which had been a Friday because I'd wanted to give her a chance to recover. Usually, Ursula hadn't worked at the hotel on the weekends which had meant that she would therefore have a full three days off before she'd be expected to return and those three days I had hoped would at least give her a chance to rest. Essentially, since Ursula had been employed as a cleaner the search for Vince had gone above and beyond her job description and had lain well outside the scope of her usual duties and so I had fully appreciated that fact and the reality that she had probably been quite traumatized by the discovery that I'd made that day.

The next few hours of that day had gone by very quickly as Ursula had left the premises in tears and then I had rapidly returned to my office in order to start the notification procedures that I'd agreed to with the local authority with regards to their clients. A phone call had immediately been made to the police to notify them that Vince's body had been found and once the police had arrived about fifteen minutes later, I had then escorted them through the building and had led them out into the back garden and towards the shed. Although a multitude of questions had been asked as we had walked, all of which I had possessed none of the actual answers to, I'd tried to be as helpful as possible due to the extremely serious nature of their visit. Deep down inside myself however, as their questions had pierced my mind I had felt a heavy weight of guilt upon my heart which had related to my own failure to keep an eye on Vince and my failure to search the whole building the very first day that he had disappeared and although it hadn't been my actual responsibility to do so, for some reason, I'd still felt as if I should have done more.

One very large question had lingered inside my mind however, once Vince's body had been taken from the shed and his remains had begun their journey towards the morgue as midnight had approached and that question had related to whether Vince had died of natural causes, some kind of medical condition or if some kind of foul play had occurred upon the premises. Unfortunately, since Vince had no longer lived and breathed when I had found him earlier that evening, there had been no way to ask him for any information or further clarity about the events that had led up to his departure from life and since his fate and destiny had ended in such a solitary manner, no one else at the hotel had been able to answer any questions about that departure in any capacity at all. A police officer had asked me that night if I had known anything about Vince's medical history or who could have been responsible for his death and I had just shaken my head because the reality had been that I had possessed very little information about any of the hotel guest's medical history unless they had chosen to share that information directly with me which Vince certainly hadn't and I'd also known very little about any of the guests movements outside the building itself.

Sadly, and tragically that day, I had finally discovered that Vince's life had ended and that his journey through life had come to an actual end but as I'd prepared to settle down for the night, I had found a little bit of comfort in the knowledge that he had been a fairly pleasant chap and so our journey through life had at the very least, been reasonably pleasant. Life as I had already known, came and went and those who remained had to soldier on regardless of what had happened and despite what had or hadn't occurred but as I'd prepared to rest, I had reflected upon my own involvement and the things I probably should have done and had failed to do as I'd sworn that from that day forth, if anyone went missing at the hotel in future, I would definitely conduct a search of the premises the very first day that I noticed their absence.

Although I hadn't been able to furnish the police with any information regarding Vince's death at the time, just a few days later I'd finally discovered from the officers involved that Vince had committed suicide via an assortment of drugs that he had intentionally taken to end his life. The sad, tragic news had really shocked me at the time because it hadn't even crossed my mind for a second that Vince might have been so depressed or so troubled by life and his worries that he had actually sought to end it himself. Part of me had crumbled for a few days after that discovery and I had walked around almost like a zombie as I'd just gone through the motions of life as I had attempted to process and cope with that sad reality and make some kind of sense of it but my heart had definitely felt very heavy due to that painful truth that I'd had to accept but couldn't really, fully understand. Deep down inside I had wished that Vince had reached out to someone and that he had asked for some kind of help, sought out some encouragement or asked for some kind of assistance but he hadn't and so he'd slipped away from the world in an empty, sad, solitary silence.

Once I had been equipped with the facts, I'd then spoken to the local authority about

Vince's departure from life, since he had been one of their clients and I'd just been a provider of accommodation which had meant that either they or his next of kin had been responsible for the collection of his belongings and his funeral arrangements. The housing allocations officer that had been assigned to the hotel, a man named Mike had not minced his words throughout our conversation as he had rapidly reassured me that someone from his department would visit the hotel to collect Vince's belongings the very next day and although it had been a sensitive matter, his tone had sounded sharp, cold and hard but that hadn't really surprised me because from my brief past interactions with Mike, his harsh attitude had always been consistent and so had almost been expected.

In fact. from the very first second that I had met Mike, a short, abrupt man with a thick, dark moustache and stocky build, I'd realized that protocols and adherence to regulations had been far more important to him than politeness or courtesy. Due to my lack of experience and my lack of any prior involvement with the local authority, I had tried to keep quite a low profile with Mike since he had generally seemed to be very harsh and extremely rigid but on occasions at times, interactions had been absolutely necessary and totally unavoidable due to the fact that I'd a hotel to fill and an agreement that the local authority could actually fill it. Over the years Mike had allocated most of the clients to the hotel and quite often those clients had been clients that no one else had particularly wanted to house, due to a number of social or more specifically antisocial issues but as I had learnt very quickly from my dealings with him, Mike really hadn't given a dam about social etiquette and all he had cared about had been the performance of his own role which had been to get people into whatever accommodation he had been able to find and secure.

One of the first and definitely one of the most memorable clients that Mike had assigned to the Happyvale Hotel hadn't in fact been one client and had in fact, actually been a couple called Cherie and Noel. The couple it had transpired had been married for at least a decade before they had even stepped foot inside the hotel's walls and despite their individual faults and human imperfections, their marriage had it seemed been built upon a firm bedrock of love from the bricks of mutual appreciation which had then been cemented together with tons of tolerant adoration and so their devotion had accumulated into a very solid, united, romantic partnership over the many years that they had walked through life side by side. Although the couple had been assigned to the hotel for temporary housing, I had been notified by Mike from the outset that they would probably not move from the hotel for a period of at least two or three years due to some very complex housing issues that had arisen which had affected their situation but I hadn't been bothered by the long term commitment, since it had offered a degree of stability and they had seemed like pleasant enough individuals.

Unusually however, the couple had been the source of one of the strangest problems that I had faced in those early days because both members of their marital union and romantic partnership had been extremely large and so some of the hotel furniture which had pretty much just been standard had been unable to cope with their individual weights and their combined mass. After several bed breakages, a few chair breakages and several furniture replacements, I had finally had to surrender and had called in an actual carpenter to actually make a special bed and a couple of chairs for the couple that could endure their daily and nightly wear and tear but the local authority, rather annoyingly, hadn't reimbursed me for the cost of the special furniture or for any the breakages that had occurred.

Unlike the jovial couple however, whose problems had merely revolved around furniture, several other local authority guests had caused me some huge issues in those early days and not all of those problematic issues had been as gentle to my mind as the bed breakages that had resulted from Cherie and her husband's occupation of a guest room. In fact, as I now reflect upon some of those early incidents, I realize that the bed breakages had really been quite pleasant in comparison to some of the other instances of drama and had merely been a pinch of salt because some of the other guests had brought far more trouble to the hotel's door and had unpacked bags of drama that had been far worse.

Towards the end of the fourth month of my hotel ownership, one of the trickier issues that had arisen had been due to a local authority guest and their conduct outside the premises which had even resulted in several complaints from a member of the public. Since multiple complaints had been made by the same person, coupled with the actual nature of the complaints, I had been deeply troubled at the time because this particular issue had revolved around Pervy Pete, a nickname given to Pete by the locals due to his creepy, perverse behavior and rightly so because his nickname had fully reflected and had totally summed up his very warped, deeply perverse nature and what he had truly, actually been.

Due to Pete's perverse conduct a local woman called Sylvia in her late forties had visited the hotel more than once in the first four months of my hotel ownership in order to discuss with me how Pervy Pete had not only physically followed her but also had virtually, sexually assaulted her. The nature of Sylvia's complaints and Pervy Pete's conduct had absolutely horrified me and so I had struggled to provide Sylvia with an adequate response on the first few occasions as I'd wrestled with shock but on the final and fourth occasion as we had sat inside my room and makeshift office, I had finally advised her to proceed with any legal proceedings that she had felt necessary as I'd listened to her horrific renditions of the events that had actually occurred.

"Mr. Gethin, he followed me home one night. He pushed me into the bushes and then he grabbed one of my breasts." Sylvia had explained. "And that wasn't even the end of it because after that he started to masturbate in the bushes. I ran away as soon as I could get free but it was very scary. Since my family knew your mother personally, I decided to let you know first before taking any further action, purely as a gesture of courtesy."

"Thank you for letting me know Sylvia." I had replied as I'd sat and listened to her speak. "When it comes to the hotel guests and their conduct outside the building, I'm afraid there's not really much that I can do. I could ask the local authority to move him since he is one of their clients but I can't control his actions outside these four walls. If it had happened on the premises then that would have been different because then I could have called the police immediately myself."

Despite the woman's very legitimate complaints and Pervy Pete's filthy, perverse, disgraceful behavior, since he had been a local authority client I had felt extremely unsure as to how I should actually react at the time because private clients had differed vastly in the sense that I had been able to throw them out straight away, if I had needed or wanted to. According to the conditions however, that I had agreed to with the local authority, their clients differed in the sense that before I could throw them out the local authority had to be notified and then if they agreed and deemed it to be an acceptable termination of occupancy, the client had to be moved, once they had managed to find an alternative, suitable form of accommodation for them to live in. The fact that Pervy Pete had been a local authority client had therefore placed me in a very awkward position with not only Sylvia but also with the other hotel guests who ultimately, actually had to live alongside this creepy, perverse sexual predator but my hands had been tied at the time by the legal agreements that I myself had entered into.

"If it happens again Sylvia, you should call the police immediately." I had finally advised her. "He's not my responsibility and neither are the things that he does when he's outside these four walls. You shouldn't feel intimidated by him and you should treat him just like a stranger because to you that is exactly what he is. My mother would not have accepted that kind of behavior from any the guests in her hotel and so, you should not accept that behavior from any man on the street, no matter where they live."

"Okay, I'll do that Mr. Gethin thanks." Sylvia had replied as she had begun to stand up. "Like I said though, being that our families have known each other for decades, I just wanted to let you know first so that if I have to call the police, you won't be surprised when they turn up at your door."

Just a few minutes later I had seen Sylvia off to the front door and as she had bidden me farewell and then vacated the premises, I'd hoped that the local authority would agree to move Pervy Pete as soon as possible because that would at least, perhaps provide some small grains of comfort to her mind and to her heart. However, as I had also realized at the time, quite possibly, Pervy Pete had been placed at my hotel because he had been ejected from a few other accommodation provisions for exactly the same reason and due to the same perverse behavior and so that possibility had deeply troubled my mind.

The horrific experiences that Sylvia had been through since Pervy Pete's arrival at the hotel had continued to weigh heavily upon my thoughts for the remainder of that day and so I had contacted Mike the very next morning to discuss the issue with him and to see if I could eject Pervy Pete from the hotel's interior. Much to my total dismay however, Mike had been quite unwilling to move Pervy Pete and certainly not straight away and that is when it truly struck me that the Happyvale Hotel had become a dumping ground for some of the most problematic clients in Camden and that I had been lumbered predominantly, with those that nobody else wanted to house or touch in any capacity at all.

My initial baptism into hotel ownership hadn't quite gone as smoothly as I had initially hoped it would and the hotel certainly hadn't been as financially lucrative as I'd hopefully considered that it would be but once the first six rocky months had passed by, I had finally started to accept that the hotel which had been handed to me quite unexpectedly, had actually become my sole responsibility. Some stormy days and rocky years definitely lay ahead of me and that reality I had truly known as I'd finally begun to understand that what I had seen my mother do for so many years and had always taken for granted had been a very hard crawl along the bottom of a deep chasm of stress in life that had been filled with problematic worries, dramatic headaches and stressful dilemmas. Although the admission of local authority clients had smoothed over some of the financial gaps, it had been a very hard baptism into a very hard customer base and a total disaster in so many ways and that reality, I had been absolutely unable to deny because time and time again, I'd had to cope with the ramifications and fallout of my own decision but failure had been such a hard pill for me to swallow and so, I had dug my heels in stubbornly, refused to accept defeat and had decided to soldier on.

THE THIEF

Over the next six months or so I had taken in more local authority clients, despite my negative experiences with Pervy Pete because to be perfectly frank, I hadn't really had much of a choice since my hotel had to be filled up and the financial pressures of hotel ownership had weighed heavily upon my mind. In accordance with our agreement the local authority had continued to send me their clients and I had continued to provide them with basic accommodation and one such client that much like Pervy Pete had also provoked a very negative response from the locals in that time period had been an Italian man who I had provided a double guest room to because he had been a married man but the negative response in this instance had been for very different reasons. Unlike Pervy Pete who had utterly repulsed me, Mario had just rubbed me up the wrong way and although I hadn't initially been able to quite put my finger upon the reason why I had disliked him so much, his character had quickly unpacked itself and his vices had then been fully revealed to me via his actions which had rapidly caused a ripple of upset within the local community.

In terms of who Mario had been as a person, he had presented himself to anyone that had given him the time of day as a cocky, confident, arrogant, brash man but I had met many people with such attitudes even during my mother's period of hotel ownership and so he hadn't really been unusual in that respect. The defensive wall of indifference to obnoxious, rude and unlikable people that I had built up over the years however, had been totally demolished by Mario upon arrival, purely due to his extremely offensive nature but that hadn't been the only problem with Mario or the only issue with his occupancy of a double guest room at the hotel.

Due to Mario's light fingers within a couple of weeks after his initial arrival there had already been multiple complaints from several local shopkeepers and even some from a few individuals and so not long after Mario had arrived, I had personally given him the nickname, The Italian Thief as my initial instincts about his shady character had rapidly been confirmed. Throughout the first few months that Mario had stayed at the hotel, one local shopkeeper had come to visit the hotel at least five times to complain and since that local shopkeeper had been a friend to my family for decades, his behavior and disrespect had irritated the hell out of me. In fact, whenever I had set eyes upon Mario's face or had just been around him for more than two seconds flat, he had irritated the hell out of me but being that he and his wife had been local authority clients, I'd had to cope with his disrespectful attitude and his behavior with a huge dollop of tolerance, even though I had longed to get rid of him from the very first second that I'd clapped eyes upon him.

Apparently and according to the complaints I had received, Mario had seemed to steal anything that he had touched and although each complaint had been noted in his resident file as soon as each one had been made, I'd been at a loss for words when it had come to the actual victims of his thievery and had been totally unable to assist them. Since each incident of theft had occurred outside the premises, my hands had been tied because I had absolutely no control over a guest's conduct once they had exited the premises and had ventured out into the local community.

From my point of view, I had definitely felt around that time that a discussion with Mario about the thefts would be highly unlikely to make any kind of difference purely due to his dismissive attitude and very sharp, sarcastic, offensive tongue but on one occasion I had decided to brave the potential verbal storm and had decided to confront him anyway. Much to my total annoyance and absolute disgust however, when I had finally raised the issue with Mario one day, after numerous complaints had been received, he had simply shrugged his shoulders and had flicked some specks of dirt from his sleeve as he'd simply shrugged and flicked off each accusation off as if each one had simply been dirty bits of dust that had not belonged to him. Apparently and from what I had clearly been able to see that day, Mario had appeared to have absolutely no qualms about what he had done to anyone and he hadn't even seemed bothered that so many complaints had been made about him.

Another issue that had been brought to my attention by one of the parties that had complained had been Mario's utilization of a local pawnshop to fence the stolen goods that he had managed to steal. From what I had been able to establish, Mario had developed some kind of rapport of sorts with the local pawnshop owner and so his venue had become not only an outlet for the goods that Mario had stolen but also a reliable source of cash for Mario's pocket but once again, since the theft and the pawnshop had been situated outside the building's four walls, I had been powerless to intervene. In the end, I had finally had to advise some of the local shop keepers to speak to the pawnshop owner and to threaten his business with legal action, if Mario persisted but as I'd been fully aware at the time that hadn't been an actual solution to Mario's thievery because there had been a pawnshop in every high street in every borough of the city and so I hadn't doubted for even a second that if one door of cash had closed to Mario, another would simply be approached.

For the entire first year of my hotel ownership, every single day at the hotel had been filled with drama whilst I had tried to manage the establishment because without my mother's firm, experienced hand at the helm, absolute chaos had absolutely prevailed and the problematic vices that guests like Mario had brought along with them and then unpacked had just been the tip of that very jagged iceberg. In many ways, it had almost felt as if I had become a duckling that had been thrown into a lake in an attempt to force the creature to swim but the major difference had been that my feet hadn't been built to paddle and I certainly hadn't been able to tread water very well and the threat of drowning in the mass of problems that had lurked above my head every morning and throughout the many sleepless nights had remained ever present. Each guest had it seemed, brought along their own bag of troubles with them when they had initially arrived at the hotel's front door which they had then quickly unpacked and as they had offloaded those problems straight onto my shoulders, every problematic issue had landed upon my doorstep with a hard, rocky bump and I had been expected to cope with and resolve every single one.

Somehow however, deep down inside, I'd felt that I had to try to save the hotel and myself, despite the thousands of difficulties that had seemed to exist and despite my lack of skills, total ignorance, absence of experience and very limited knowledge. Although I had been shoulder deep in the problems that I'd never expected to cope with, never mind actually be held responsible for as each day had gone by, the depth of the hotel's problems certainly hadn't reduced and if anything, the problems had actually grown far deeper and so at times, I'd definitely feared that I would drown in the mass of difficulties. Despite all the chaos however, I had persevered and soldiered on through the drama as I'd drunk a bottle of wine each night and the odd stiff glass of whiskey a few times a week as I had attempted to try to understand the hospitality industry and the how it actually functioned.

When it had come to the actual issue of the hotel's administration, the bureaucracy had been a total nightmare from start to finish that had never seemed to depart, end or tire and as I had faced the mountain of issues in the form of paperwork that had waited for me every single morning, that nightmare had continued but rather sadly, I'd been fully awake. Every day tricky, complex administrative tasks had to be performed, many of which had related to the local authority clients and it had been a web of complexity that I had been totally underequipped and absolutely unable to deal with and so the paperwork had fallen behind and had rapidly mounted up.

Much to my total dismay, the problems that I had faced had not just been internal however, as the hotel had continued to attract the worst kind of attention from the local area which had become particularly problematic to me one morning towards the end of that first year. My Friday morning had started off pretty much as usual as I had eaten breakfast and then performed my usual routine building checks but as I'd returned to the hotel's main ground floor hallway, I had heard a sudden, very loud knock at the front door.

Once I had opened the front door, much to my surprise, I'd found a male upon the hotel's front doorstep that had looked like a drifter that had seemed to be in his late fifties with dirty, dark brown, matted hair and in every way imaginable, it had definitely felt rather strange at the time because I had never ever seen him before. In every sense of the word the man had been a total stranger to me and as far as I had known, he hadn't been connected to any of the guests that had stayed in the hotel at that time or since my period of hotel ownership had begun and so I hadn't recognized even a single strand of the matted clump of hair that had sat upon his head. Despite the man's very rough external appearance and his unexpected visit however, I had quickly plastered a polite smile across my face as I'd prepared to listen to him, if only for a minute, in an attempt to provide him with a ounce of respect which I had doubted that he'd seen very often, due to the very strong, totally repugnant aroma that had emanated from his being.

"You got a room for me?" He had asked.

"No sorry, we're full at the moment." I had immediately replied as I'd shaken my head.

Just for a second or two, I had actually considered that perhaps I should invite him inside and allow him to take a shower and that maybe I could provide him with a spot of breakfast and a fresh set of clothes but a room had been totally out of the question because at the time, the hotel guest rooms had all been fully occupied. However, much to my total surprise and shock, before I had even been able to arrive at an actual conclusion and decision that might have gone in his favor, less than a minute later things had rapidly taken a turn for the worse.

Suddenly, just behind me, I had been able to sense Ursula's presence and as I'd begun to wonder if his hair had truly been that color naturally, or just darkened by the dirt that he had so obviously lived in, Ursula had poked her head out from behind me and had become visible to the man which in retrospect, probably hadn't been the wisest thing to do on her part. Rather shockingly and extremely disturbingly, the man had it seemed, suddenly noticed the actual presence of a woman and so he had quickly walked down the steps, rapidly pulled down his trousers and then lain down on the ground.

In order to protect Ursula's eyes as the man had started to roll around the cement walkway and had reached for his penis to perform a very sexual act of public masturbation, I had quickly closed the front door as a gasp of horror had slipped from my lips because he had done all these things in the middle of a very public street. The closure of the front door I had hoped at the time, would perhaps serve as some form of deterrent because it would deprive him of an actual audience and it would also perhaps give him less of an incentive to continue which I'd hoped would be a sufficient enough form of action to put an end to his perverse display.

Upon my face there had been a very confused expression as I had turned to face Ursula, then offered her an apologetic but nervous smile and had shaken my head but I'd been able to see from her horrified expression that she had been truly shocked and probably had felt just as shocked as I had. Since the man's sexual behavior had been so very public and so very unexpected, an awkward silence had lingered between us both for a few seconds as we had remained inside the hallway, glued to the spot and unable to utter a single word and it had almost felt as if we'd both been scared to break that silence because that would mean an actual discussion about we had just seen.

For once, I had been completely caught off guard and had been totally knocked off balance and so for a few more seconds, I'd allowed that awkward silence to uncomfortably occupy the air inside the hallway between us because to be perfectly frank, I hadn't really known what to say to Ursula or exactly how to respond. Although we had both remained by the front door, it had almost been as if we'd been frozen to the spot by total shock and as if our tongues had been tied up in awkward, uncomfortable knots of discomfort because our lips had remained tightly shut and for once, even I had been absolutely speechless as my mind had remained lost for words for at least another minute.

"Well that's not a very nice way to introduce yourself." I had finally joked as I'd attempted to break the very uncomfortable silence that had not only slipped into the hotel's entrance but that had also made itself quite comfortable as it had sat between us both almost like a verbal barrier.

"Yes, that was absolutely awful." Ursula had mumbled in agreement. "It was a very ugly sight for very sore eyes."

Just a few seconds later, thankfully for us both, Cherie had suddenly bounced cheerfully into the hallway and as she had smiled at everyone present and nodded her head, she'd asked us what all the commotion had been about because the man outside had been very loud and rather noisy and so, she had actually noticed the disturbance en-route to the communal kitchen on the ground floor. Once I had explained the situation to Cherie, unlike my reaction which had been to immediately shy away from the man's presence and his vulgarity, much to my absolute amusement, Cherie had then rapidly opened up the front door and had actually boldly stepped right out of it and then to my complete surprise, she had even started to scold and ridicule the semi-naked man with a bold tongue, a scornful expression and a mouthful of verbal courage.

"Is that all you got Mister?" Cherie had teased as she had laughed very loudly at him. "Put that shabby, little thing away. Really, it's so tiny, you can't be showing that thing off."

The uncomfortable silence and awkward conversation that had filled the hallway prior to Cherie's arrival had then suddenly, been totally dismissed and shattered into a thousand pieces of hilarity as Ursula had released a huge fit of giggles and I had sighed with sheer relief. Upon the man's face there had been an expression of absolute confusion and surprised shock as he had glanced up at Cherie's face, instantly ceased his masturbatory activities and then had just lain completely still upon the ground. Another few peals of very loud laughter had been released from Cherie's mouth and then she had even pointed towards the man's exposed body parts as she had begun to boldly deliver another portion of humiliation directly to his ears and as I had watched and listened to her in total amusement, I'd almost burst into a fit of laughter myself.

"Look at that isn't it so funny?" Cherie had boomed to a passerby. "Can you imagine having to cope with that small thing every night?

Due to Cherie's bravery and her very courageous attitude the man had it appeared, rapidly become even more embarrassed and as I had watched him start to cover himself up with his dirty tracksuit bottoms once more, I'd chuckled in absolute delight and with total amusement. Just a few seconds later I had watched in amused silence as the man had begun to put his clothing back on again and it had definitely seemed as if the verbal embarrassment that Cherie had delivered straight to his ears had truly shocked him and had even made him feel quite ashamed. Quite unexpectedly, the man who had obviously expected everyone around him to be startled, shocked and intimidated by his strange perversion and his vulgar behavior had instead, suddenly been humiliated and embarrassed himself and that unpredictable turn of events had not only tackled but had also dealt with his inappropriate behavior head on.

"Mr. Gethin, I think we should ask some of the guys to come out here and get them to show him what a real penis should really look like." Cherie had jokingly suggested in a very loud voice.

Not more than a few seconds later and once the man had crawled along the ground for a few meters in order to slightly distance himself from the building, much to my total satisfaction, I had then watched him fully retreat as he had quickly picked himself up of the ground once more fully clothed. A satisfied smile had adorned my face as I had continued to observe his movements and he had begun to walk briskly away and as soon as he had been out of earshot, I'd immediately congratulated Cherie on her smart wit and her courage.

"Well done Cherie and thank you so much, his naked body parts were not a pleasant sight at all." I had said appreciatively as I'd smiled at her and then gently patted her on the back. "You certainly handled him and you gave him a proper verbal kick up the butt which he actually, really needed."

"Yes Cherie, you're so brave." Ursula had agreed as she'd smiled. "I couldn't have said or done anything like that."

"Don't worry about it Mr. Gethin, it was nothing really." Cherie had replied as she'd grinned. "Some guys just get out of hand sometimes."

"Still that naked display was a bit too close, a bit too public and a bit too sexual for comfort and for my liking." I had concluded. "So, I'm really glad you were around."

"At least he's gone now Mr. Gethin." Ursula had said with a sigh of relief. "A bit of distance at times, can actually be a good thing."

"Yes, a bit of distance from his shabby bits is definitely a good thing. In fact, I'd take a cruise around the world just to get away from those." Cherie had joked.

Ursula had giggled. "If he does that

everywhere he goes, I'm not surprised he's an outcast." She had thoughtfully concluded. "Usually, I feel sorry for people that are down on their luck but not for him that was a truly disgusting, absolutely filthy display."

"An outcast, I'd call him more a dreg of society and he really is right at the very bottom of humanity's deep barrel of human decency." Cherie had replied. "I mean seriously, there are lots of homeless guys out there and most of them don't behave like that."

"I agree ladies." I had replied. "I just hope he doesn't come back."

"What an absolutely foul thought." Ursula had mentioned as she'd shuddered. "Totally and utterly foul."

"Still, it is an actual foul possibility." I had considered.

"Yes Ursula, you should sprinkle some bug repellant all over the hotel's front steps." Cherie had jokingly suggested. "To keep him and his foulness at bay."

Ursula had giggled.

Once all the commotion from the repugnant, strange man's masturbation act had died down and once my normal day had resumed once more, unfortunately as I had rapidly discovered, peace had not been due to be an actual guest at my hotel at any point in that particular day. Another dramatic issue had raised its ugly head just after lunch and had frustratingly presented itself to me but the next chaotic issue of my day that day, much to my surprise, had come to my attention when I had suddenly heard some very loud screams that had emanated from the second floor which had been instantly recognizable to me because each one had come directly from Cherie's mouth. Since every problem inside the hotel had been my sole responsibility, I had quickly dashed up the stairs towards the double guest room that she had shared with her husband Noel in order to establish the reason for her screams because each alarm filled one had sounded extremely urgent.

When I had arrived outside the couple's room, I'd immediately found Cherie on the landing in a very disturbed, distressed state and she had rapidly pointed towards the interior of the couple's room and so I had then quickly entered into the room as she'd politely held the door open for me. From what I could see at first glance as I had stepped inside the room and then given the interior a quick visual scan, there had been no apparent visible reason or logical explanation to account for Cherie's shaken state and so I'd glanced at Noel's face to seek further enlightenment but he had simply shrugged in response which had clearly indicated to me that he'd been just as confused about Cherie's upset as myself. Just a second or two later however, Cherie herself had entered the room and as she had begun to walk towards us both, words had started to tumble from her lips along with a few sorrowful sobs which had accompanied each stammered, blurted, panic-stricken explanation as she'd attempted to explain her distressed state.

“Mr. Gethin, I just saw a rat; it climbed onto my bed and then sat there right in front of my face and ate a carrot." Cherie had explained hysterically. "It was absolutely huge Mr. Gethin with jet black fur and white razor-sharp teeth."

"Where did it go?" I had asked.

"Somewhere over there." Cherie had explained as she had pointed towards the skirting boards in one corner of the room.

Since Cherie had been a well-known food hoarder, in some respects, it hadn't really surprised me that if a rat sighting had occurred somewhere inside the building that such a sighting would have taken place inside her room because if a rat had managed to find its way into the building, Cherie's room would definitely be its first port of call. In fact, if I had been a rat or even a mouse in search of a regular meal and a food rich place to live, the couple's room would have been my ideal home too because the two had been known to not only consume but also to hoard stacks of food on a daily basis inside their shared guest room.

An element of uncertainty had however, lingered inside my mind and had clung to my thoughts as I had rushed across the room and then had begun to search the corner in question as I'd started to inspect the skirting boards more thoroughly and search for any signs, hairs or sounds from the creature.

Although a hole had existed that had definitely been large enough for a rat or a mouse to squeeze through, at that time I had felt slightly unsure as to the validity of Cherie's rat sighting claims because even though I'd inspected the area very carefully, there had been absolutely no signs to back up her words and not even a hair or whisker had been spotted, present or found, much to my absolute frustration and total confusion. Despite all my doubts however, I had taken the issue very seriously as I'd swiftly returned to the center of the couple's room and then had turned to face Noel once again, just to see if he could perhaps shed any further light upon the matter, since after all he had been inside the couple's room with Cherie at the time of the supposed rat sighting.

A huge worry had definitely lingered inside my mind at the time as I had visually searched Noel's face for any answers but all that had greeted me had been total silence and so that worry had silently somersaulted around inside the passageways of my mind without the provision of any kind of comfort to buffer its chaotic turbulence because as I'd already known, Cherie's claims had massive financial implications. Several issues had flooded to the forefront of my mind as I had considered the matter more thoughtfully, such as the possibility that a whole family or pack of rats may have found their way inside the building because as I'd known, it had been highly unlikely that a solitary rat had travelled alone and then entered the hotel's four walls, the possible need to fumigate the whole building, and the issue of the couple's actual food storage inside their guest room. From what I had known at the time about rats and mice, such creatures tended to travel in groups and so it had been highly likely that if a rat had managed to find a way to enter inside the building, there would be more than one and more than one problem. Since the whole floor and perhaps even the entire building might have been infiltrated by rats, the issue had really worried me as I had begun to search for answers more carefully once again but still no signs of the solitary creature that Cherie had claimed to have seen had been present.

"Did you see the rat Noel?" I had finally asked as I'd paused for a moment and then turned to face her husband.

“I didn’t see a thing Mr. Gethin, but I was having a nap and I am quite a deep sleeper.” Noel had rapidly clarified.

Inside my mind, a few doubts had still lurked because no guest that I had known off had ever seen a rat before inside the hotel and so I'd begun to wonder if perhaps Cherie had just been in the middle of a nap too and that perhaps she'd had a nightmare that had somehow involved a rat which had scared her and woken her up. Since Noel had been in the bed right beside Cherie and he had seen absolutely nothing, I had found it hard to be absolutely certain that it had not just been a bad dream but for the next twenty minutes or so, I'd waited around inside the couple's room just to see if the rat would reappear in order to comfort Cherie and provide her with the reassurance that I had at the very least, taken her rat sighting extremely seriously.

The whole issue of a rat invasion had very serious implications and so for my own as much as Cherie's sake, I had treated her claim with the seriousness that the matter deserved, regardless of its validity, because as I'd already known, a rat infestation would cost a lot of money to eradicate and so I really had to be absolutely certain. A visit to the hotel from a Pest Control company as I had been fully aware at the time, would cost a very large sum and that money would not be well spent, if the rats didn't even exist in the first place and so before I spent any money and made an attempt to resolve the problem through extermination and elimination of the actual vermin, I had to first be very sure that the creatures had darkened the hotel's door and that the rats had made a home inside the building's interior.

"How come you're so brave with human beings but so scared of rats Cherie?" I had asked as I'd finally prepared to leave the couple's room.

"I just don't like them Mr. Gethin, they bite people when they're asleep." Cherie had replied.

"Don't worry Cherie, if there are any rat residents inside this building, I'll soon kick them out." I had immediately reassured her. "They won't occupy my hotel for very long, though in the meantime, you might want to make sure that you don't leave any food lying around because that would be helpful. Rats and mice tend to gravitate towards and live of any scraps of food that they can find and so your room would be considered a prime and highly sought-after location on any vermin's food radars."

"Yes, you're absolutely right Mr. Gethin, I'll try to be more careful in future." She had immediately reassured me with an obedient and compliant nod.

Just a few hours later, when I had finally concluded that my day might become slightly calmer, since no rat had yet appeared or shown their face again, I'd finally begun to relax as I had prepared to settle down for the night and consume my evening meal and my usual bottle of wine. Although I had still remained quite anxious to establish whether or not a family of rats had decided to occupy my hotel as I'd already known, nothing could be done until another rat sighting had actually taken place and had occurred. Due to the usual daily stress from the hotel and its occupants, my evening bottle of wine had become almost like a medicinal requirement to me to help me through each day and night which I had usually consumed alongside my evening meal but unfortunately for me, just as I'd been about to settle down and enjoy my evening, another dramatic event had suddenly taken place but this time, it had involved one of the guests that I had actually really, totally loathed, Mario the Italian Thief.

Suddenly, a verbal alarm had sounded out which had almost knocked my ears out of their sockets in the form of a very loud scream which had emanated from the first floor but this time around, it had come from Betty's lips and lungs. The notion of a peaceful evening meal had quickly fled from the forefront of my mind and my pleasant thoughts had rapidly abandoned me, chased away by the noise that had truly alarmed me and so as I had immediately leapt to my feet, then dashed out of my room, I'd begun to make my way towards the first-floor landing. Once I had arrived upon the first-floor landing, I'd found Betty, a quiet, middle aged, mild mannered woman in a shaken, disturbed state but the disturbance on this particular occasion however, much to my total disgust, had not been caused by any external third parties, or even by any unwelcome animalistic guests like vermin and had very sadly, I had rapidly discovered, been caused by another hotel guest.

When Betty had verbally related to me the reason for her shaken state, I had instantly been shocked, disgusted and absolutely horrified because another guest had created that drama and done something to Betty that day which as far as I'd been concerned had been absolutely unforgivable. The guest in question that had caused all the drama that evening, I had instantly disliked from the very first moment that he had initially arrived and had stepped foot inside my hotel, purely due to his sarcastic nature and shifty character which had always irritated the hell out of me, In fact, every time I had spoken to, or even just seen Mario, his attitude had always really grated me but so far and up until that point in time, I'd had no legitimate reason to boot him out of my hotel and so I had just had to tolerate his presence inside the hotel's four walls with a grin and bear him.

Since Mario and his wife, both of whom were Italian had been given a double room further along the hall on the same floor as Betty in some ways, the couple had virtually been Betty's neighbors but according to Betty that neighborly proximity had caused her more drama than anything else and on that day in particular it had actually, resulted in an actual theft from her room. Due to Betty's distressed state, I had remained totally silent as I'd listened to her accusations against Mario and as I had done so, I'd thoughtfully considered that there might actually be a legitimate reason to kick him out for good and that possibility, I have to admit, had slightly cheered me up.

“Mr. Gethin.” Betty had complained in a nervous stammer as she had sobbed. “Mario took my necklace, the one that my mother bought for me. I left my room unlocked earlier, just for a few minutes when I went to the toilet and by the time I had returned, the necklace had gone and then just now, I saw his wife wearing it."

Once I had established all the facts, due to

the commotion, Betty's upset and her accusations all of which had required an immediate response and remedy, I had then immediately rushed along the hall towards Mario's room and had happily given the door a very sharp, loud knock as I'd prepared to confront him to his face, straight away. In some respects, to be perfectly honest, the situation had held some positive prospects for me because it would perhaps furnish me with a legitimate reason that I could then perhaps utilize to justify his permanent ejection from the hotel either that day, or at a later point in time and so I had felt really quite optimistic about it, despite the negative events that had taken place.

In terms of Mario's age, according to the records that I had kept inside my resident's files, he had been in his mid-forties at the time and his wife had been around the same age and since they had been allocated to the hotel as longer term residents that would stay at the hotel for a period of at least six months and possibly even up to a year that had meant that they hadn't been in a rush to leave, much to my dismay and irritation. Due to the more permanent nature of the couple's occupancy that had also therefore meant that an actual push might be required in order to encourage them to permanently vacate the premises and to encourage the local authority to move them and so as I had stood in front of Mario's door and prepared to confront him, I'd thoughtfully considered that reality prospect and how I could perhaps usher in their departure from the hotel more rapidly because Mario had already brought a lot of trouble and complaints to the hotel's front door.

A few seconds later, when Mario had answered the knock at his room door, I had then taken a deep breath as I'd glanced at his slim, tall stature as I had internally prepared to verbally tackle him head on. Although I had felt slightly intimidated by Mario's physical presence at the time because he had towered way above my head, somehow, I'd managed to dig deep within myself to muster up some seeds of courage and a few drops of bravery though sometimes even now, I still wonder if perhaps some of those drops of bravery had actually been formed from the fearful sweat upon my brow.

"Betty's necklace has gone missing Mario and your wife was seen wearing it." I had demanded in a stern tone and firm voice. "I don't tolerate any kind of theft inside my hotel and especially not from other guests."

"I just found the necklace on the floor in the hall Mr. Gethin and so I gave it to my wife, so that she could look after it." Mario had immediately replied as he'd swiftly shaken his head in denial. "I didn't even know who it belonged to."

Although Mario had professed his innocence to me and he had totally denied the accusations, deep down inside myself, I had definitely felt at the time that every word that he had uttered to my face and ears had been a total lie. Since no one had actually seen Mario enter inside Betty's room however, it had been hard to challenge him further on the matter because it had simply been Betty's word against his and if I had taken Betty's side which I'd definitely wanted to at the time, I would have perhaps been accused of some kind of favoritism.

"The necklace please." I had insisted

sternly as I'd adamantly stretched out a hand towards him.

Another reluctant shake of Mario's head had immediately been given in response as he had turned and then headed back inside his room and less than a minute later, much to my total relief and partial satisfaction, Mario had returned to the door of his room with the necklace draped across and wound around one of his hands. Some traces of slight reluctance had definitely seemed to be present in Mario's facial expressions I had noticed as he had handed the necklace, seemingly quite begrudgingly, back to Betty who had stood quietly just behind me and not a single word had been uttered by either of the two as she had silently accepted its return with a disgusted expression upon her face. A relieved, appreciative smile had been politely offered to me by Betty as she had turned to face me and so since the matter had been resolved to some extent, I had started to prepare to return to my room but even the actual resolution I'd definitely felt at the time had fallen far short of what Mario had really, truly needed which had been a good, firm kick up the backside.

"I'm watching you Mario." I had warned him as I'd pointed sternly towards his tall, slim, lanky frame. "Very closely, very closely indeed."

Not another word had been spoken by the tall, shifty thief as Mario had quickly turned around and then had simply gone back inside his room but he had banged the door shut behind him which I still remember had really irritated me at the time and as I had watched him scarper, I'd shaken my head in total disgust due to his absolute foulness. Unfortunately for me, on that particular occasion, I had been unable to pin Mario down by his shifty, dodgy tail but I had still found some grains of comfort in that the fact that at the very least, a suspicious event had actually taken place and had finally occurred because that event I had felt, might possibly come in handy at a later date and could even help me to finally get rid of Mario for good.

Due to the upset that Mario had caused that day as I had walked Betty back towards her room door, I'd tried to reassure her that I would see if I could swap her room around and move her to another floor as soon as possible and a floor a distance away from Mario's light fingers. Although the issue of Mario's thievery had not actually been settled that day, I had at least been able to take some comfort in the knowledge that Betty had been given her necklace back which had meant that the cherished piece of jewelry would not end up in the local pawn shop on the high street since that had been the usual outlet that I had known Mario often frequented, especially when he had wished to fence stolen goods.

No doubts had lain inside my mind however, as Betty had thanked me appreciatively for my assistance with a grateful smile and I had left her side to return to the ground floor, about the actual issue of the necklace and its disappearance from Betty's room because I'd definitely felt that Mario had stolen it which had meant, a very sharp eye had to be placed and kept upon him from that point forward. Since it had transpired that day that Mario had no actual respect for the place where he had lain his head each night, or for any of those around him, I had continued to worry about his presence inside the hotel as I'd returned to my living space, my bottle of wine and my evening meal because there had been no immediate remedy to that particular issue.

"Mario's a trouble maker." I had advised myself as I'd sat down beside the small, wooden table inside the kitchen area of my room which had also served as a lounge, a bedroom and an office. "And he's not even a polite, respectful thief that steals from only the rich, he'll steal from anyone, even from someone poor like Betty." I had muttered to myself under my breath as I'd shaken my head in sadness and then had begun to consume my now lukewarm evening meal.

Unfortunately, one absolutely huge thing had been highlighted to me that evening through Mario's disgusting behavior towards Betty however, and that one huge thing I definitely had to process very quickly because the evening had truly enlightened me and shown me that some of the long-term guests inside the hotel could present problems to not only me but also to each other. Due to Betty's rather timid nature, Mario had perhaps incorrectly assumed that she would not raise the issue with anyone and object to the theft but she had challenged him and since she'd done so successfully, she had even managed to retrieve her necklace from his light fingers and she'd even alerted me to the fact that Mario had and would steal from other guests, if the opportunity presented itself to him.

Another question had continued to linger inside my mind that night however, and it still bothered me even after I had consumed my usual bottle of wine as I'd lain inside my bed and prepared to rest and that had been whether or not Mario's wife had known the true origins of the necklace when she had accepted it from him. Since Mario's wife had not appeared at the door of their room earlier that evening, throughout the actual confrontation with Mario, there had been no way for me to gauge the likelihood of her possible involvement in the actual theft itself and so I had begun to speculate, assume and accept that she had probably accepted the necklace from Mario in total ignorance.

The presence of one definite, known thief in the building had been greatly preferable to me than the possibility of two potential thieves and although the piece of jewelry had been wrapped around Mario's wife's neck that day which had meant that Mario had been unable to deny that the necklace had been in his possession that hadn't necessarily meant, I had finally concluded as I'd closed my eyes that his wife had known about the necklace's origins. In some ways, that assumption had been made more to appease my own mind than anything else because that assumption had been easier for me to accept and easier to fall asleep with and so I had fully accepted it as I'd waited to drift off into the gentle arms of slumber.

A heavy, weary, defeated sigh had escaped from my lips as I had waited for slumber to embrace me and carry me off into the peaceful arms of the night as I'd continued to mull over the chaotic shenanigans that had once more visited my hotel that day. The usual glasses of wine that I had drunk that evening and my evening meal hadn't been fully enjoyed when I had returned to my lounge that night, purely due to Mario's thievery which had left a sour, bitter aftertaste in my mouth.

Unfortunately that day, a very harsh, extremely loud wakeup call had been delivered directly to my mind when it had come to the issue of guests like Mario and so I had been under absolutely no illusions at all that from that point forward, the hotel and my management of it was not going to be a holiday camp and that I really had to step up to every single challenge because if didn't, no one else would. Although Mario had been given another chance that evening because if I had really wanted to I could have kicked up more of a fuss, called the police about the theft and then just kicked him out, however I'd slightly feared the repercussions of more severe action being taken on my part because he really had been such a shifty character. Deep down inside myself, I had always hoped that Mario would leave one day through his own volition and off his own accord but that evening had shown me that a voluntary departure may not actually be likely and that one day soon, I might have to force his actual exit.

Once the next morning had arrived and breakfast had been consumed, I had then briefed Ursula on Betty's room change and I'd instructed her to assist Betty and to help her move her belongings before I had discussed the possible rat sighting in Cherie's room.

“It might have just been a nightmare Ursula.” I had explained. "But we have to be vigilant now and on full alert because rats are a very serious health hazard."

"What an eventful day and night Mr. Gethin." Ursula had replied as she'd rapidly nodded her head in agreement. “Don't worry, I’ll keep my eyes open just in case.”

Since the hotel had five floors with three guest rooms on each floor, it hadn't been difficult to find a room and a willing occupant to exchange with Betty because some of the floors further up the building had housed guests that had been all too willing to move closer to the ground floor. Once Betty had been moved around and Ursula had returned to her usual cleaning duties and routine, I had then performed my usual building checks which I had normally performed each day in the morning at around eleven but much to my surprise I had heard another shriek from Cherie again although this time it had come from the bathroom on the ground floor.

Just like the first time around, I had immediately rushed to assist Cherie and as another loud scream had emanated from her mouth, I'd begun to knock upon the bathroom door and then had quickly entered the room because although she had been a female guest, I hadn't waited on this occasion for her permission to enter, purely due to the urgency of her screams. This time around however, I had found Cherie semi-naked in the middle of the bathroom with a bathrobe held up against her body that had barely even covered some of her most essential naked body parts being that Cherie had been a bit on the large side. Out of respect I had rapidly held my head to one side and then had partially covered my eyes as soon as I'd entered the room and had noticed her semi-naked state, to try to avoid the sight of Cherie's naked layers of skin which had protruded from the robe that she'd tried to hold up against her body in an attempt to cover up her flesh.

Some drops of water had been sprinkled across Cherie's arms, I had noticed as she had stretched one of her arms out and then pointed towards a corner of the bathroom which had clearly indicated to me and implied that she'd been so badly shaken that she had not even had not had a chance yet to dry her skin. Fortunately, by this point however, Noel had made his way downstairs, much to my total relief, since her semi-nakedness had been slightly uncomfortable for me because she had been a married female guest and I hadn't wanted anyone to feel that I would take advantage of another man's wife.

Once on the scene, Noel had immediately put his arm around Cherie's shoulders as he had tried to calm her down which had relieved me to some extent because it had been quite difficult to establish exactly what the problem had been up until that point because all that had come out of Cherie's mouth had been her shrieks of distress. Since Cherie had been in such a shaken state when I had arrived, she had not yet managed to verbally explain the reason for her distressed state but fortunately, Noel's arrival on the scene and his presence had instantly seemed to soothe Cherie and calm her down which had been extremely helpful. In terms of Noel's stature, he had been a large man but despite his large size, he'd possessed a quiet, calm, sensible nature and a very soft voice and he had always seemed to be the calmer of the two in that particular marital coupling and in this instance, his calmness seemed to touch, appease and soothe Cherie instantly.

"Cherie, Cherie it's fine now. I'm here now." Noel had reassured her as he had picked up a nearby towel and then had begun to wrap it around some of her exposed body parts.

Cherie had sobbed as she had nodded her head. "I saw the rat again Mr. Gethin and I definitely saw it, right over there." She'd continued as she had pointed towards a corner of the bathroom. "It came out of the skirting boards and then it scurried across the bathroom floor, bold as brass."

Much to my absolute relief, the presence of Noel had at least seemed to have calmed Cherie down a bit and his huge frame, sensible demeanor and calm hands had somehow, gently nudged her out of her shaken state which had then meant that she had been able to release a few words and that she had finally been able to discuss the source of her distress. Due to Cherie's size as I had already known, she had to utilize the bathroom on the ground floor, if she wished to shower or bath because to be perfectly frank, the hygiene facilities on offer in the other bathrooms on the other floors of the building, simply hadn't been large enough to comfortably accommodate her physical needs, since the bathtubs had all been the same standard size and so she had come down to the ground floor bathroom that morning as per usual. The ground floor bathroom had a much bigger bathtub and even had a shower facility inside it because it had been far larger which had meant, Cherie had been able to comfortably do whatever she had wished to inside that bathroom and so that morning, she had followed the usual structure of her daily hygiene routine but the second rat sighting had been far from usual and so naturally, she had raised the alarm.

For the second time I had diligently inspected the skirting boards which had been the area of the alleged rat sighting in a dutiful manner but once again, I'd wondered about the validity of Cherie's claims because absolutely no one else had seen any rats inside the hotel except Cherie up until that point in time. Partially, I had begun to wonder if perhaps Cherie had just seen a dark spot on the ground which had then triggered some mental images of a rat that had related in some way to her first rat sighting which had possibly been attributable to a nightmare but I'd had no real certainty about that possibility either. Since no one else had seen a rat yet, I had remained quite unconvinced and since I myself had not even seen a whisker or even a hair that had belonged to a rat, I'd remained slightly skeptical, purely due to the lack of visual confirmation and lack of other sightings. Due to Cherie's nature which had been as I already known, quite excitable coupled with her tendency to exaggerate, it had been hard for me just to accept her sightings and claims as absolute truths and I'd have greatly preferred if such claims had been validated by at least one other human source and another set of human eyes.

"Cherie, no one else has seen any rats yet."

I had started to explain as I'd discussed her rat sighting further. "I need to have at least one more sighting by someone else before I can call in the exterminators."

"Mr. Gethin, when I started to scream the rat ran away and then it totally disappeared." Cherie had insisted. "You believe me right Noel?" She had asked as she'd turned to face her husband.

"Sure, Cherie but I understand what Mr. Gethin is saying, he might have to fumigate the whole building and that will cost a lot of money and so, he has to be absolutely sure." Noel had explained.

"Exactly." I had agreed as I'd nodded my head.

Fortunately for me, Noel who had also utilized the ground floor bathroom regularly for exactly the same reason as Cherie, due to his own physical constraints had thoughtfully considered my position and he had come to a very sensible conclusion that had fully aligned with and supported my own because I had to at least justify the cost of a visit from some exterminators to myself. Just as I had given the bathroom another quick visual scan however, just to see if I'd missed anything, much to my total surprise, I had noticed a plate full of snacks on top of a nearby laundry basket. Part of me had almost chuckled out loud as I had silently considered Cherie's snackful habits which had it seemed, gone everywhere that she had gone and even the bathroom it had transpired, hadn't been exempt from her huge appetite.

"You really shouldn't bring food into the bathroom Cherie." I had advised her as I'd pointed towards the plate full of snacks. "It really doesn't help, especially if there are rats inside the building."

“I know Mr. Gethin and I apologize but I definitely saw a rat twice now.” Cherie had insisted.

"I'll have to see what I can do Cherie." I had finally promised her as I'd nodded my head. "Leave it with me."

Some doubts had continued to linger inside my mind as I had begun to wonder why no one else had seen any rats because I'd definitely felt that if there had been rats inside the interior of the building, someone else should have seen one by that point in time. One thing had however, leant in Cherie's favor and that had been the fact that her compulsive eating habits had meant that she'd be more likely to attract such vermin wherever she had gone because she'd always be around the desired food and scraps that rats and other vermin had been likely to gravitate towards. Everywhere that Cherie had gone around the building as I had already known, there had always been food and so if rats had existed and had been present, it had made total sense that the creatures would follow Cherie around everywhere she went. A viable explanation for Cherie's solitary rat sightings had in the end existed and as those satisfactory but far from pleasant thoughts had passed silently through my mind, I had begun to consider the possibility that I might actually have to call the exterminators in anyway, just to put Cherie's mind at rest.

A final glance had been cast back towards the offensive skirting board and the corner of the room where Cherie had insisted the rat had been before it had vanished and once again, I had noticed that there had been an actual hole large enough for a rat or mouse to squeeze through and so her claims had seemed possible and even quite plausible. Although a part of me had still remained uncertain as I had nodded my head at the couple politely as I'd prepared to vacate the bathroom, deep down inside I had known at the time that a visit from the exterminators had looked increasingly likely and that it had sat just upon the horizon of the next week and so I'd released a frustrated sigh as I had left the room because as I'd also known that visit certainly wouldn't be cheap. Nothing particularly happy had seemed to exist inside the Happyvale Hotel and that reality had begun to wrap itself around my body and mind throughout the rest of that morning as I had glumly carried on with my routine tasks because the name of my hotel made absolutely no sense to anyone and especially not to myself but for the very first time, I'd started to accept that very grim reality.

COMPULSIVE CHERIE

Since I had assumed control and ownership of the hotel, a huge issue for me had been the various insects that had infested the premises to some extent but after Cherie's initial rat sightings, it had seemed as if rats had decided to jump into that equation, become far more stable guests and had enthusiastically joined that array of wildlife due to an increase in the number of sightings. Unfortunately, that following week, the rat sightings had definitely grown but unlike the initial two sightings that had occurred however, the other sightings had taken place in other parts of the building and had not involved Cherie at all and may have involved the same rat or several different rats. Due to the increase in rat sightings, the rat's presence had become not only far more obvious but also absolutely and totally undeniable to anyone that lived inside the building and so towards the end of that week, I had prepared to call in a pest control company.

According to Cherie's lifestyle which had involved an immense amount of food and consumption of that food in every place that she had gone in that respect, Cherie had presented me with more than just a few problems because food and Cherie had it seemed, been totally inseparable. In terms of Cherie's weight, she had been always been extremely overweight and her appetite had been, from what I had seen of it, absolutely enormous and so food had been hoarded and stored in every single inch, nook and cranny of the guest room that she had shared and occupied alongside her husband that it possibly could have been. On several occasions, I had even taken the time to explain to Cherie how her food storage habits had a direct impact upon the vermin and pest problems but that hadn't seemed to dissuade her and it certainly hadn't changed her habitual desire to hoard whatever food she had been able to lay her hands on inside the couple's guest room.

"Cherie, you just can't leave food lying around." I had explained to her several times. "Rats, mice and cockroaches will start living inside your room and then that will become everyone's problem, not just your own."

Several times in the past, when we had held such discussions, Cherie had mentioned to me that at times when she had felt hungry and tired that she'd often struggled to get dressed and then go all the way downstairs to the kitchen and so throughout that week, due to the additional rat sightings, I had started to consider the actual purchase of a small fridge for the couple's room as a possible solution. Whether I had liked it or not, Cherie's compulsive eating habits which had involved the excessive consumption of food coupled with her total lack of discipline when it came to the actual issue of food storage and the vermin problems had all been issues that would not just disappear and so the pest control measures I had felt in the end, would not really be sufficient and that it would only be a matter of time before more vermin returned.

The reality had been as I had been fully aware that Cherie had been such a huge source of food for the creatures that had usually scurried around in the underground tunnels underneath the buildings of the city each day and night that those food scraps had attracted them to the couple's room. Due to those very persistent factors at play, I had definitely felt that such habits, if allowed to continue, would just attract the same kind of attention from vermin again at some point in the future and so I'd known that further preventative measures had to be taken. However, the decision to purchase a small fridge had essentially been an extremely difficult one for me to make because I had at the time, also felt very concerned about Cherie's weight and health and had absolutely no desire to encourage the food binges that had bubbled away just below the surface of her human flesh. In the end however, due to the escalation in rat sightings, I had finally had to take into consideration the health of the other guests and since rats, mice and cockroaches were not generally good for anyone's health, I had finally decided to make an attempt to reduce the risk of any unwelcome guests in the form of vermin upon the premises with the provision of a small fridge.

Although in some ways it had been against my better judgement at the time, purely due to Cherie's weight, the fridge I had planned would be placed inside the guest room that Cherie and her husband shared and that measure I'd hoped, would minimize the scraps of food lying around inside their room. For me, the small fridge I had felt had been a compromise that would liberate us both to some extent and although it hadn't been the ideal solution for Cherie's individual health, I had finally succumbed to Cherie's wishes to store food inside the couple's guest room and her huge appetite, purely out of necessity.

Once a pest control company had visited the hotel and the small fridge had been bought, delivered and had been placed successfully inside Cherie's room by the delivery men, at the start of the next week, throughout the Monday afternoon, I had planned to go through some of my paperwork in my lounge where there had been a small office area. Due to my successful resolution of some large problems that the hotel had faced over that past couple of weeks, my mind had been slightly more relaxed that day because I had not only managed to cope with all the issues but had also to some extent, even overcome them and so I had felt really quite optimistic about the day and the week ahead.

Usually, I had performed all my paperwork seated at the mahogany desk in the small office area inside my lounge and although I refer to it as an office, it had been more of a corner of my lounge really and so as per usual that Monday afternoon, I'd sat down in front of my desk as I had prepared to face the mountain of paperwork that had required my attention. The small area that I had allocated to the hotel's general records and storage of those records had been quite basic really and hardly even qualified to be considered as an office at all but it housed a few folders upon the shelves above the desk and there had also been some paperwork and stationery items tucked away inside some drawers of the desk itself. Although the provisions had been very basic, the facilities had definitely sufficed over the years since the hotel hadn't been particularly large which had meant, it had only required a handful of commercial suppliers and there had only been a couple of actual permanent employees.

Just as I had sat down to start work however, suddenly there had been a very loud knock at the front door and since the knock had sounded quite official and extremely loud, I had immediately dropped everything and then had rushed out of the room and into the hotel lobby to answer it. Very strangely, when I had actually opened up the front door, much to my total dismay, once again I had found the same strange man on the other side of the door that had created a huge fuss in the past when he had performed some acts of very public masturbation upon the hotel's actual doorstep.

Not even an ounce of embarrassment had seemed to exist on the man's part and he appeared to be totally unapologetic about his last appearance which had of course involved, a very naked exhibition as he had stood boldly and confidently upon the doorstep of the hotel.

Due to the man's sudden, very unexpected second appearance, I had quickly taken a deep breath and then held my breath as I'd braced myself for another potentially awful run-in with him, though exactly what form that run-in might take on the second occasion, I had at that time been unable to foresee or predict with any degree of accuracy.

For some inexplicable reason it had seemed, this very weird man had developed some kind of strange fascination with the hotel which had made absolutely no logical sense to me at the time because no one as far as I had been aware had ever encouraged him to visit the building. Yet once again, bold as brass, this strange man had shown up without an invitation and he had put in a very personal appearance and so as I had held my breath, I'd stood completely still almost like a statue of frozen uncertainty as I had silently tottered around on the brink of fear as I'd waited for him to speak.

"You got a room for me?" He had asked as he'd vigorously clawed away at his body.

Much like the man's first visit, he had asked

me the same question again and although when it came to the issue of actual issue of hotel occupancy, on this particular occasion there had been a vacant, single room, due to his bodily infestation which I had assumed could be lice or fleas and his past behavior, I had felt very reluctant to offer that accommodation to him. Some kind of insects had seemed to be present on his body and inside his clothing from what I had observed on his second visit because he had clawed away at himself as if he'd been infested which had been another reason on top of his past naked display that I'd immediately refused to accommodate him and had rapidly begun to shake my head in response.

A guest that had been covered in bugs as far as I had been concerned, could and would contaminate the whole building and his past display had been enough to put me off housing him right from the very get go and so at the time, it really hadn't been a hard decision to make. The fact that the man had returned however, had surprised me immensely and his boldness had totally caught me of guard and so I'd hesitated slightly before I had finally managed to squeeze out an actual verbal response to his question.

“Sorry, we don’t have any rooms at the moment.” I had finally nervously blurted out and my words had almost stumbled over each other as each one had fallen from my lips and out of my mouth due to my worries about what might happen next. "We're all full up."

Just as I had begun to shut the front door however, as I'd prepared to return to my office in order to get on with my afternoon and complete the paperwork that I had to attend to that day, something even more strange had then taken place as the man had released a very loud cough. Due to my anxious curiosity I had immediately opened the door back up, although sometimes even now, I really wish I hadn't because an absolutely foul sight had instantly greeted my eyes. Much to my absolute horror and total disgust, the second time I had opened the door, I'd found the man crouched down on the hotel steps with his soiled, filthy tracksuit bottoms around his ankles and as he had stared me straight in the face, he had then begun to take a dump on the actual doorstep of my hotel.

The sheer cheek and audacity of the strange man's actions had instantly made my blood boil and as I had stood and watched him, every part of me had silently seethed inside as I'd felt a current of intense anger surge chaotically through my veins which had threatened to spill out of my mouth and explode from my human frame because his brazen, foul nature had completely horrified me and absolutely disgusted me. Fortunately, once again however, Cherie had ventured downstairs for one of her frequent, daily kitchen visits to prepare and load up on some cooked food and as I had heard her approach, I'd immediately turned to face her. Despite Cherie's hunger because she had of course been en-route to the actual kitchen, she'd instantly spotted me stood by the front door and she had also noticed the strange man again and so fortunately for me, she had then begun to take a slight detour as she had started to walk towards us both with an amused smile upon her face.

In many ways, the sight of Cherie had

instantly soothed me because just her very presence alone had somehow, slightly pacified me and the amused expression upon her face had rapidly taken the edge of what had been a very uncomfortable moment. Luckily, Cherie had managed to capture my attention and distract me from the anger that had surged through my veins like a current of total hatred as much like a cool bucket of water, her presence had extinguished some of the fiery, angry flames inside of me, due to her cheerful disposition which had immediately put me slightly at ease and so a tense, strained smile had somehow, managed to surface and then take a stroll across the lower part of my face as I had faced her.

"Oh, he decided to visit us again Mr. Gethin, I think he likes us." Cherie had teased. "Do you need some toilet paper Mister?" She had then called out as she'd addressed the man directly.

From deep within myself, a bubble of laughter had suddenly erupted due to Cherie's hilarious comment and funny question as I had attempted to see the humorous side of the situation and had gratefully appreciated her sudden appearance, her very bold response and her courageous direct approach. Prior to Cherie's arrival on the scene however, to be perfectly frank, I had been absolutely horrified, totally shocked, extremely angry and completely mortified by his defecation upon my doorstep and so her comical attitude and playful verbal jabs had definitely helped to shake me out of my stationary but emotionally turbulent, very angry state.

Although I had expected Cherie to be more disgusted than I had been because usually as I had been well aware at the time, females didn't generally like to discuss men's toiletry habits, never mind actually spectate whilst men performed such bathroom rituals in front of their faces, she had once again blown me away with her sheer bravery and light-hearted attitude towards life and the disgustness of some of the people in it. Somehow, it had transpired, Cherie had been totally immune to this filthy man's outrageous behavior and she had not only challenged him but also grabbed him verbally by the rump and then fully delivered some shots of direct embarrassment to his absolutely foul tail and her tactful response to his foulness had definitely amused and pacified me to some extent.

Despite the fact that the hotel's front steps had by this point been totally polluted with faeces, somehow Cherie had managed to lighten my mood but as I had also realized at the time, she had probably cared far less about the mess because the responsibility for that foul mess hadn't been one that would fall upon her shoulders. Just a few seconds later, much to my sheer relief, another guest had also joined us and had waded into the murky depths of the foul situation as the big Irish man Tom who had been another long-term local authority client had suddenly sauntered down the hotel hallway towards the open front door. Once Tom had arrived at the doorway, he had then come to a complete standstill as he'd glanced at both Cherie and myself and then he had looked at the strange man on the doorstep of the hotel with a slightly amused but bemused expression upon his face.

“What’s going on Mr. Gethin?” Tom had asked.

Quite frankly, I had been totally lost for words at the time, partly due to the shock of it all and partially because an attempt to explain the strange man and his disgusting antics had just seemed to be a very complicated issue to verbally delve into and so, I'd just shaken my head in response. A very confused expression had crossed and adorned Tom's face as I had watched him silently absorb the scene and the man who had continued to participate in his dump on the hotel steps and my own face which had been riddled with a look of total frustration and absolute disgust had offered no verbal explanation as my lips had remained totally silent and I'd simply offered him another defeated shake of my head in response. However, Cherie, who had rarely struggled for words and who probably could have spoken for the whole of Camden, at this point had suddenly decided to verbally jump into the conversation and so she had then decisively attempted to provide Tom with a very thorough but quite comical answer.

“Look out there Tom, there's a man pooing on the doorstep with no toilet paper.” Cherie had pointed out as she had giggled and then pointed towards the man on the steps outside. "And last time he came here, he even showed us his tiny bits."

"Who is this man Mr. Gethin and why is he taking a dump on the doorstep?" Tom had asked as he had popped his head out of the doorway, glanced at the man and then shaken his head.

“I have absolutely no clue Tom. He just showed up here one day and now it seems, he wants to keep coming back.” I had replied.

“I think he likes the hotel Tom.” Cherie had piped in. "So, this might even become his main, regular pooing spot and his preferred masturbation location."

"Do you need me to handle this Mr. Gethin?" Tom had asked as the expression on his face had suddenly changed to a frown and he had rubbed his hands together. "I can take care of this sewage bag in a jiffy." He had reassured everyone as he'd taken a step forward and then had begun to enthusiastically roll up his sleeves.

For a moment, I have to admit, I had been

tempted to allow Tom to beat the filthy man to a pulp because the man had really scared Ursula and he had continued to disrespect my hotel and the guests that occupied it, not just once but on two separate occasions with his dirty antics. However, part of me deep down inside had definitely feared the actual damage that Tom had the physical capacity and potential to deliver to the man's physical frame and that fear had constrained my immediate response as my decision had lingered indecisively in my mind, unmade and totally avoided for a brief moment in time. No doubts had existed inside my mind that day that if Tom laid a hand upon the strange man's human body, he would in all likelihood end up in a hospitalized state and that he might even perish in a dirty street corner somewhere because no one would even want to assist him since he had looked so disgustingly filthy and had smelt so horrendously foul.

"Mr. Gethin, what would you like me to do?" Tom had urged. "I really think you should let me handle this for you right now. I can get rid of him quite quickly and I'm sure that if I do that today, he'll never come back here ever again."

Suddenly, the man had stood back up and he had then begun to pull up his dirty, soiled tracksuit bottoms and his actions had rapidly jolted me out of my thoughts and my indecisive state of paralysis as I had swiftly been pulled back to the sordid, filthy reality. An urgent realization had rapidly struck my mind that the moment to act and make a decision about the dirty man on the hotel steps had fully landed upon my doorstep of life and so that decision as I'd realized at the time, had to be made immediately.

"He definitely didn't use any toilet paper Mr. Gethin, yucky, yucky, yuck." Cherie had joked as she'd started to giggle.

Initially, although I had felt totally disgusted by the strange man's conduct, Cherie had expressed nothing but amusement however, thoughts of the future had plagued my mind and had been full of worries for me because this man had been a nuisance at that point in time, on two separate occasions. The very negative pattern of behavior that this man had it appeared, decided to engage in I had felt would only continue on a downward spiral and it had seemed highly unlikely that his behavior would change and he hadn't just been a nuisance, he'd also been a very dirty nuisance. Technically, because the man hadn't been an actual guest at the hotel the option to throw him out hadn't existed and he hadn't even been a visitor either which had meant, he couldn't actually be banned from the building and so I had struggled to make an immediate decision because it had been a very difficult decision to make.

Although the filthy man hadn't at that point, even stepped foot inside the premises, he had caused more trouble and commotion just outside the building with his two external visits than the majority of guests and their visitors usually had inside it and his disrespect had irritated me profusely. Deep down inside myself, a few worries had definitely lurked which had related to the possibility that he might show up again and that I might have important visitors on the premises when he did so like safety inspectors and so on because I had been due to meet with an official later that afternoon and so that particular issue had worried me immensely as I'd silently wrestled internally with my decision.

“Leave him for now Tom and if he comes back again, I’ll let you know and then you can do whatever you want to him.” I had finally replied.

"Okay Mr. Gethin but I think you better at least let me scare him away today." Tom had insisted. "Just a little bit. If I don't, he might come back again quite soon and next time he might do something even worse."

"If he can do anything worse but I think he's already hit rock bottom on the scale of filthy behavior." I had concluded. "Okay Tom go ahead, just a loud shout or two should do the trick."

Tom had nodded.

“You see Mr. Gethin, you really are quite soft.” Cherie had teased. “Someone else would have just gone out there and chased him away with a baseball bat.”

Due to my desire to get rid of the nuisance who had it seemed, decided to make Happyvale Hotel his regular stop off point as quickly as possible I had finally agreed to allow Tom to intervene, albeit with just a couple of loud, verbal threats but I'd really felt quite reluctant to allow Tom to actually cause the strange man any kind of physical injury on that particular day. Although I had tried to scare the strange man away myself the first time he had shown up with a curt attitude and hostile response, it didn't seem to have made a scrap of difference, nor had it appeared to have had any effect upon him at all and so as I'd already known, something else really had to be done and done immediately.

Since Tom's voice had definitely been far louder, much rougher and a lot deeper than my own, I had predicted that it would be interpreted as much more of a threat by the unwanted visitor and so I'd hoped that a few verbal shouts and threats would in the end, do the trick and keep the unwelcome guest at bay. The opportunity that Tom had offered to me had in the end been to good to pass up on completely and to scare the strange man away just a little, I had finally decided, wouldn't cause too much commotion or inflict too much harm upon him because after all he had taken an actual dump on the hotel's steps which had been an actual health hazard in itself. A deep fear had occupied and lingered in my mind at the time that if I had failed to act in some way that day, the man would simply return within a week and that then he would probably do something far worse and I had dreaded to imagine what a manifestation of that something far worse might possibly be because in my opinion, he had already sunk to the lowest levels of human behavior already.

Just a few seconds later I had begun to watch in total silence as Tom had embarked upon his mission which had been to chase the dirty man away from the entrance of the premises with verbal threats and as a scowl had crossed Tom's face and his fists had flown up into the air, some very loud, angry words had darted from his mouth like verbal arrows of anger. The filthy man had immediately glanced at Tom and then much to my sheer relief and total delight, after one fearful, nervous look, he had then hit the streets in a hurry and had begun to scurry off. Deep down inside myself at the time, I had totally understood the strange man's very abrupt retreat and rapid departure as I had watched him quickly scarper with his tail between his legs because Tom had really been a total beefcake of a man and had been built like an absolute powerhouse of muscular flesh.

Once all the commotion at the front door had died down, I had then immediately sought out Ursula and some disinfectant because the man had left the five steps that led up to the hotel in a very dirty, totally foul state and his disappearance, certainly hadn't cleaned up that mess or solved that immensely filthy problem. Just a few minutes later I had returned to the hotel steps along with Ursula who I'd managed to track down very quickly and as I had returned to the scene of disgust, I'd been armed with a large bottle of disinfectant that I had managed to collect en-route.

"Ursula, we have to clean this mess up straight away I'm afraid." I had urged as I'd pointed towards the disgusting piles of mess that had littered the stone, concrete steps.

Each step had looked utterly filthy, purely due to the bodily excrements that had lain across each one and the foul mess had made it hard to enter or leave the building without a foot being placed upon something disgustingly nasty and so the mess had to be dealt with not only straight away but also very thoroughly. Fortunately, however, Ursula's attitude had been very understanding and she had immediately given me a compliant nod and then had rushed off towards the cleaning cupboard to collect some more cleaning products as I had begun to splash some disinfectant over the five steps. Just a few minutes later Ursula had politely returned armed with a shovel and a piping hot bucket of frothy water in her hands that had seemed to contain some very powerful cleaning products and I had immediately noticed that she'd also collected another very large bottle of disinfectant en-route which had immediately reassured me that the mess on the steps would not remain intact for very long.

"Right on that hygienic note Mr. Gethin, I'm off to the kitchen to make some mid-afternoon snacks." Cherie had suddenly mentioned as she'd glanced at the cleaning products, smiled and then had shaken her head. "Do you want anything to eat?" She had asked politely.

"You might be hungry once you've cleaned up all that stinky mess."

"No thanks Cherie, I'll be fine." I had replied as I'd attempted to remain totally focused upon the steps and the mess that had been dumped on each one. "Once I finish up here, I have some paperwork to attend to which I have to complete today."

Approximately twenty minutes later and once all the mess had been cleaned up, I had then made my way back inside the building and had sauntered towards the communal guest kitchen and as I'd stepped into the very basic, small area which had adjoined a slightly larger guest lounge, I had found Cherie still inside the room. Upon one of the kitchen worktops I had immediately observed there had been a huge amount of food and that food had literally been heaped up onto two plates as high as the two food piles could have possibly gone, both of which I had immediately assumed would be consumed shortly by both Cherie and her husband. An amused grin had almost crossed my face as I had silently absorbed Cherie's potential food consumption that afternoon which had comprised of a bunch of baguettes filled to the brim with cream cheese and rashers of fried bacon, some pizza slices and even some chips that had been freshly fried along with various other edibles.

"Cherie, those are snacks?" I had teased.

"Well Mr. Gethin, it's just a spot of second lunch really for Noel and I." Cherie had replied with a cheerful smile. "We usually have our second lunch around about now. We're generally quite big eaters because as you can see, we have a lot of space to fill." She had joked.

"Why do you need a second lunch, are you skipping dinner tonight?" I had asked since my curiosity had by that point, definitely been aroused.

"No Mr. Gethin, we usually have two lunches per day and dinner every evening because one lunch is not really enough to fill us up until dinner time and so mid-afternoon, we tend to have our second lunch." Cherie had explained. "I'll make dinner in a couple of hours' time, so this lot is just to keep us going until then."

The sight of the mountains of food that had occupied the two plates had intrigued, amused but also in some respects, slightly shocked me because I couldn't have consumed that amount of food in a whole day. Nonetheless, the two huge piles of food had all seemed quite natural and very normal to Cherie I had observed as I'd watched her pick up the two loaded plates just before she had begun to make her way back towards the couple's guest room and her husband.

Later that afternoon as arranged and expected, at four on the dot an inspection officer from the local health and safety regulatory body had attended the premises to inspect the condition of the accommodation provisions offered to guests at the hotel as per the conditions that I had agreed to when I'd accepted guests funded by the local authority. Usually, the inspection officers had paid me a visit once every six months and when they had attended the premises to conduct their inspections, they had normally asked me all kinds of questions and then written down lots of little notes upon the notepads that had been clipped to their clipboards as I had given them a tour of the premises and so I had felt quite relieved that at the very least, the strange, filthy man had by that point, totally disappeared. Unlike a stranger that usually doesn't ask too many questions in order to avoid being too intrusive however, the safety inspectors' questions as I had already known tended to be very sharp, abundantly plentiful and painfully precise and since I had no explanations for the man's filthy behavior or his strange fascination with the hotel fortunately, that had been one less drama to cope with and attempt to explain throughout the inspection officer's visit.

Due to the palaver earlier, that day I had almost dreaded the inspection officer's scheduled appointment and physical appearance that afternoon but fortunately, since the filthy man had vacated the entrance of the hotel and abandoned the entire street, his foul mess hadn't been something that the inspector had been able to find fault in. Approximately one hour after the inspection officer's arrival, he had left the premises with his notepad and clipboard and luckily, the recent rat problem which had already been handled to some extent had somehow, escaped his notice and hadn't been raised as an actual issue on that occasion which had relieved me no end and so as the early evening had stepped into the heart of the city, I had then returned to my lounge and living area to relax for the evening. After all the commotion earlier that day, a pleasant, quiet evening spent with my evening meal and my usual bottle of wine had been a very welcome prospect indeed and so I had been eager to enjoy and savor that potential calmness and forget about the filthy storm that the strange male visitor had brought to the hotel's front door.

A couple of hours later and well after the inspection officer had vacated the premises, I had begun to settle down inside my own lounge with my evening meal which had not only been a lounge and a makeshift office but which had also housed a small bedroom area at one end of it and a small kitchen area. My evening that day, I had planned to spend with a cheerful bottle of wine and my dinner which I'd by this point, actually prepared and then cooked in the kitchen area of my room and I had hoped that it would be uneventful because a bit of peace and quiet had been extremely desirable.

Upon my face there had been a peaceful smile as I had sat down and then started to eat, drink and relax as I'd let the shenanigans of the day peacefully melt away because as I had already known, the next day's drama, chaos and problems would definitely show up again the very next morning and I would be expected to cope with whatever life and the hotel guests decided to throw my way. Since I had assumed responsibility for the hotel, I hadn't actually had many peaceful moments to myself and so I'd tried to find some small grains of comfort in the calmness of my evening and the first moments of that day that I'd have truly all to myself.

After a few hours of peaceful relaxation, I had then begun to make my way to bed with a cheerful smile upon my face because my bed had at times, offered me a comfortable zone of potential sanctuary and an escape from the hotel's drama with a pillow of peacefulness upon which to rest my often weary, very stressed out head. Once I had lain down and then closed my eyes, I'd rapidly begun to drift off to sleep, almost instantly as slumber had been silently ushered in extremely quickly, no doubt due to the active, chaotic day that I had just endured and the glasses of wine that I'd consumed alongside my evening meal. Despite all the drama that the day had contained and had brought my way, the glasses of wine that evening had definitely done the trick because sleep that particular night as I still remember had come very easily to me indeed.

Sadly, and unfortunately however, sleep had not been due to be my companion all night that particular night and my period of rest had been very short lived because just a couple of hours later, I had been very sharply and rather abruptly woken up by a huge commotion in the form of a huge crash and some screams that had emanated from somewhere upstairs. Despite my sleepy state I had immediately leapt out of bed, grabbed my slippers and robe and then I'd rushed straight out of the room and into the ground floor hallway because the crash had been extremely loud which had meant, a major calamity had occurred somewhere upon the premises.

Once I had stepped out into the main hallway, I'd then headed straight for the stairs and I had literally dashed up the first flight as I'd begun to internally prepare myself to face the disaster and the source of not only the huge crash but also the screams. On the landing of the first floor I had found a female guest Charmaine in a shaken state and in tears just outside her room and neither Charmaine nor the door of her room which had still hung open had offered any kind of explanation to me which had meant, the interior of her guest room had to be inspected for further clarity. Quite naturally, I had approached Charmaine and then I'd begun to look through the open door to search for any clues that might enable me to establish the facts and what exactly had actually occurred and as I had done so, Charmaine had begun to rapidly provide me with some of the very strange details as to what had just taken place. Due to Charmaine's distressed attempt to explain the situation to me, I had then quickly abandoned any guesswork as I'd focused my attention solely upon her explanations and had started to listen to her because her shaken state really had demanded my instant and full attention.

"They just came through the ceiling Mr. Gethin." Charmaine had sobbed as she'd pointed towards the open door of her room. "They almost landed on top of me, I'm lucky to be alive really."

The source of all the trauma, distress and tears it had rapidly transpired, once I had listened to Charmaine speak and then had stepped through the guest room door had been an actual double bed that had crashed through the ceiling which had then landed upon the floor directly below it. Unfortunately, the double bed on its way down had practically crushed all of the items of furniture inside Charmaine's room in its path as it had made its descent and none of the furniture inside her room had it seemed, escaped any damage or survived from the impact of that crash. Upon the double bed two very sheepish looking, semi naked individuals sat, namely Cherie and her husband Noel and as I had glanced at them both, they had quickly grabbed some bed clothes which they had then hurriedly wrapped around their bodies in an attempt to cover up their nakedness.

"I'm so sorry Mr. Gethin." Cherie had tearfully sobbed.

For a few minutes, I have to admit, I had been totally unable to verbally respond, purely due to the devastation that had greeted my eyes which had composed of not only the state of Charmaine's room and some damage to the floor but also a torn apart ceiling that had sat directly above my head and all the items of broken furniture which of course had also included the couple's broken double bed. Unfortunately, and as I had realized at the time, it would cost an absolute fortune to repair all of the damage that had been done and that worrisome thought had crossed and occupied my mind as I had absorbed the scene that had surrounded me in shocked silence. Although a part of me had almost wanted to cry at the time, somehow simultaneously, another part of me had felt a sudden urge to laugh because the scene that had greeted my eyes had really been quite comical, albeit expensively comical.

Quite obviously, I had rapidly realized, the sheepish looking couple had been in the midst of a shared moment of passion and they had perhaps become carried away by the passion of the moment and by their own love making which on that particular occasion had not been a gentle saunter down a quiet lane of desire. Unlike the ground floor of the building which had been formed from an extremely solid, very thick block of cement, some of the other floors inside the building had not had the same kind of cement structured base and so the floor of the couple's room it had transpired, had been unable to cope with the trauma of their sexual wear and tear and more specifically, the friction from their very passionate love making. Since both members of that particular romantic partnership had been extremely overweight, the combined weight of their two physical bodies and their very vigorous love making, I'd had to quietly accept had obviously been too much for the bed and the hotel floor to withstand and so both the frictional pressure of their passion and their mass of combined weight had ploughed straight through the actual floor itself which had ultimately snapped in response.

“Yes, we're both very sorry Mr. Gethin.” Noel had added a minute or so later with an apologetic expression upon his face just before he had begun to stand up. “I'll just go and get us some clothes.” He had continued as he'd then started to head towards the door.

"Yes, that's a very good idea Noel." I had immediately agreed. “Just try to be careful and please don't go anywhere near the hole in the floor.” I'd advised him before I had turned to face his wife as I'd continued to process and absorb the scene before my eyes that had shocked every ounce of my being. "I just don't know whether to laugh or cry Cherie."

In so many ways, the entire scene had amused but also shocked me and so I had begun to question which part of the destruction directly in front of me had been more of a shock or an amusement as Noel had left the room, the broken ceiling from the couple's weight or their semi-naked forms that had just been actively engaged in some frantic acts of unbridled passion. A part of me had gratefully appreciated the fact that at the very least, the scheduled six monthly official inspection visit had already taken place earlier that day because as I had been fully aware, if it had been due to happen the next day the provision of an actual explanation for the very large hole in the ceiling of Charmaine's room would have been difficult to provide and that would have put me in a very awkward position.

Meanwhile, due to all the commotion, a few other guests had by this point gathered on the first-floor landing and some of them had even popped their heads around the door of Charmaine's room to establish the source of the commotion and what exactly had caused the very loud, huge crash that had woken them up. Upon a few of the guests' faces I had noticed that there had been some amused smiles and even a few snickers and giggles had emanated from some of their lips as they had managed to successfully, silently work out for themselves what exactly had just happened which of course had amused some of them immensely.

Once I had recovered slightly from the

initial shock, I'd then begun to thoughtfully consider how much damage had really, actually been done, how much money it would cost me to fix it a bit more precisely and I had also made a mental note to rehouse the couple in another room situated on the ground floor of the building. The couple's room had been damaged significantly and so too had the room below it and since the downstairs floor would provide the couple with a far more stable form of accommodation, I had decided to move them to the ground floor and to allow them to remain there to avoid a repetition of my past mistakes.

A very huge mistake, I had by this point realized, had been made on my part due to my lack of foresight and my lack of knowledge, when I'd initially given the couple a room on the second floor because the weaker floor and the combined weight of both Cherie and her husband hadn't been compatible at all and that night, I had learnt that very expensive lesson the hard way. The damage itself unfortunately, would not be covered by any insurance claims I had already begun to speculate because insurance companies in those days certainly hadn't covered the cost of frantic love making or any damage done during moments of unbridled passion and so the weight of the guests who had been accommodated on the weaker second floor by myself, would in all likelihood just be regarded as a reckless decision.

"Okay everyone, the circus is over so you can return to your rooms now." I had said a couple of minutes later as I'd suddenly turned to face the door and then addressed the small group of spectators that had gathered. "Some people aren't clothed properly right now so it's not very decent to hang around." I'd gently reminded the other guests. "I apologize for the disturbance to your night's rest."

From just outside the door a few more snickers and giggles had emanated from the lips of the guests that had congregated upon the first-floor landing and they had whispered amongst themselves for a few more seconds before they'd started to head back off to their rooms and as I had watched them depart, a weary sigh had been released from my lips. The consequences of the couple's over enthusiastic love making had created more than just a few problems which as I had known by that point, I'd definitely have to solve that same night and each problematic issue had lain silently at my feet as I had been left alone with just Charmaine, Cherie and the broken mess. All three guests had to be re-accommodated at least temporarily that night somewhere else in the building because both Charmaine and the couple's room had been unsafe to remain inside and that problem had presented me with an actual urgent issue to resolve.

One single vacant room on the ground floor had been kept purely for emergency intakes which would be able to accommodate either one or two of the three but that had meant that a shortfall had existed which I would have to find an actual way to plug that very same night. Some broken bits of furniture had lain strewn haphazardly across the ground and as I had taken one last final glance at the debris, I had shaken my head in total frustration because none of the broken pieces of furniture had it seemed, been able to offer me any kind of solution to the problems that had been created and the worries that had occupied my mind.

Suddenly, the amusement that I had initially felt had completely evaporated and much to my total discomfort, I'd found that all that had remained had been the financial responsibilities of repair which really hadn't looked great and had almost felt as mangled as the broken furniture. Some builders as I had already known, would have to be called first thing in the morning and so as I had waited for Noel to return, I'd begun to silently plan ahead and even started to speculate as to whether or not the floor above my head could be stabilized temporarily and the hole covered up somehow which would then mean that at the very least, Charmaine's room could be tidied up and occupied again fairly soon. For the rest of that night however, I had silently concluded as I'd watched a fully dressed Noel enter back inside the room with some items of clothing in his hands for his wife just a few minutes later, both rooms would be totally off limits to everyone inside the building because the floor of one room had totally collapsed which had also meant, the ceiling of the room below it had caved in which had presented me with a huge safety issue.

"Now that was a very expensive moment of unbridled passion." I had muttered to myself as I'd prepared to vacate the damaged room.

Since Noel had returned and had brought some clothes for Cherie with him, I had felt anxious to vacate the room immediately so that Cherie could at least get dressed, though I had still remained uncertain at the time as to where exactly I would accommodate all three room-less guests. However, as I had taken a very deep breath I'd reached deep within myself and somehow, I had managed to muster up a grain of courage as I'd turned to face the three guests and had then prepared to brave the hurdles of the night and make an attempt to actually overcome them.

"If you can all follow me please, once you're dressed of course Cherie, I'll lock up your rooms now and then I'll sort out some alternative accommodation for you to sleep in for the next few nights, just until a more permanent solution can be found." I had politely instructed the three room-less guests. "You can't sleep in these two rooms now, it's far too dangerous. A bit of love can be very dangerous it seems and do a lot of damage."

Just a few seconds later I had led two of the three room-less guests out of the guest room and onto the first-floor landing as I'd left Cherie alone so that she could put on some clothes and make herself look decent. Once I had gone upstairs and locked up the couple's guest room, I'd then immediately returned to the first-floor landing where I had found Cherie fully clothed alongside her husband Noel and Charmaine. Since I had felt at the time that the couple had definitely required more privacy than Charmaine who had been a single person, I'd decided in the end to offer them the single room and to house Charmaine in my lounge for a few nights which hadn't been the ideal solution but I had possessed a camper bed for emergencies and that I'd decided in the end, would at least provide her with an emergency sleeping facility and a decent night's rest.

Much to my total relief, once I had settled the three in alternative sleeping facilities and I'd returned to my own bed once again, the remainder of that night had slipped by peacefully enough but a shadow of financial worries had definitely hung over my heart and mind which had remained when I had woken up again the next morning. The huge mountain of financial expenditure that had lain at the foot of my bed and the hotel's doorstep as a result of all the damage that had been done the previous night as I had already known, would not be easy to climb and the peak of that mountain had loomed way above my head and well out of my financial reach. Although a new day had arrived, the worries from the previous night's events had not yet fully disappeared and as yet, I still hadn't quite figured out how I would scale that mountain, cover the financial expenses that had been incurred or whether I'd even be able to reach the top of that very high financial peak successfully.

WEEKEND OF NIGHTMARES

After a whole year had gone by and a few loans had been secured to cope with the damages to the building and guest rooms from the first year's guest wear and tear, rather frustratingly, I had begun to accept that the Happyvale Hotel had definitely become a dumping ground for those without any other housing options in Camden. Due to the financial fluctuations and difficulties that I had faced however, that had meant that there had been no other real viable alternatives or not that I had seen on the horizon of potential solutions. A tightrope of financial instability had bridged the gap between total financial collapse and me being buried under the avalanche of financial difficulties that the hotel's quasi-corporate existence had presented to me and I had managed to walk across that tightrope for a whole year without a fall and so I'd been able to at least find some small comfort in that achievement, although my achievement had been far from perfect and had even tottered upon the brink of total failure and had been much closer to an absolute disaster.

The only other real feasible option for me at that point in time and real choice that I had actually had, would have been an actual sale of the hotel itself which had been a choice that I'd been reluctant to pursue since I had wanted to respect my mother's memory and to fulfill her final wishes. However, the packed in bodies like sardines that had lined the hallways and stairs on many occasions throughout my mother's period of ownership and management had throughout that year, started to make a lot more sense to me, since I had begun to understand the commercial realities at play that my mother had faced and had to cope with. Due to my accommodation of government clients and the strict regulations that I had agreed to adhere to, the packed in sardine option hadn't been an option that I'd been able to utilize myself and so I had felt slightly restricted at times and even quite frustrated due to the constant financial pressures.

When it came to the majority of the hotel guests that I had been sent by the local authority, I'd also realized by that point that pretty much like me, they'd had no real choices in life either when it came to the roof over their head and that the Happyvale Hotel had become an urgent stop gap for many of them. Somehow, it had felt as if we had all been bundled and thrown together by the circumstances of life and then we'd had to manage those difficult circumstances and tread water in the deep oceans of hardship as best as we had been able to with no arm bands, rubber rings, life guards, life boats or rescue rafts in sight.

Quite strangely, although we had all crossed each other's paths from different walks of life, we had all had one thing in common in that we had rarely seen any glimpses of the mountain peaks of glory and our lives had predominantly wallowed in some very deep pits of stress, chasms of despair and valleys of misery and so, we'd had to learn to cope not just with those miserable depths but also with each other. The respective demons that we had usually hidden away inside each of our closets had during that first year, somehow managed to escape and had then run amok along the hotel's hallways, unconquered and unchallenged as we had wrestled with our own consciences and our close daily proximity. Although such demons would have usually been kept and would have remained hidden away from sight by the closet doors of our own ignorance and our own individual failings unfortunately, the hotel and its close living arrangements had brought each one to surface of our shared days and nights and so our usual masks of patient civility, faces of polite pretention and cloaks of tolerance had been fully stripped away by dramatic tensions, chaotic shenanigans and outlandish outbursts.

Fortunately, however, there had been one slight saving grace that had kept me rooted, focused and anchored throughout that first year to my overall objectives when it came to the actual hotel itself and that one little light in the darkness of my own ignorance, inexperience and failings had actually been Ursula the cleaner. Overall, Ursula had saved me from many hours of laborious effort and bundles of stress and I had actually inherited her commitment to the hotel from my mother's period of ownership because she had already been employed as an actual cleaner and in service when I'd assumed control and ownership of the hotel. Although on several occasions I had noticed that Ursula had made mistakes in that not only had she misplaced items but also that she had frequently left the cleaning cupboards unlocked which had meant that the contents had been pilfered many times, for the most part she'd really been a tremendous help.

In fact, as I now reflect back upon my first year of hotel ownership, I doubt that I could have coped with the hotel and with all the difficulties that I'd had to face without Ursula's support, cooperation and participation because her attitude towards the hotel, the guests and myself had always been pleasant, helpful, cooperative, humble and respectful. Countless stains had been handled competently throughout that year by Ursula's hands and the hallways, small lounge and kitchen area had always been cleaned absolutely meticulously, every single weekday. When it had come to the issue of the actual guests' rooms, so many filthy rooms had been cleaned out by Ursula, once the occupants of the hotel had finally vacated each one and she had also given so many guest rooms a light clean once a week throughout that year whilst some of the guests had still been in occupation.

A sense of gratitude had definitely grown into a huge heap inside of me during that first year for Ursula because she had not only remained committed to the hotel after my mother's departure but she had also embraced the changes in customer base, had coped with my lack of experience and had even endured the low levels of monetary compensation which really hadn't been that great. On so many occasions Ursula had even gone well beyond the duties of her actual employment contract and I had leant upon her numerous times in so many ways for support of various kinds and she had always provided me with a reliable, sturdy, patient, tolerant crutch of assistance and so that support had resulted in a deep well of appreciation within me because it had been absolutely irreplaceable.

When it came to the changes in customer base at the hotel and the acceptance of local authority clients, in terms of the actual impact of my decision, at the end of that first year things had started to settle down slightly both financially and logistically but it hadn't been an easy bed for me to lie in each night and more like a bed of problems with a bedframe formed from some large jagged rocks and a mattress made from hundreds of very hard problematic pebbles. So many financial issues had arisen throughout that first year with regards to breakages of furniture, destruction of fixtures and fittings, theft of hotel property and so on but the local authority had rarely reimbursed me for anything and had seemed to totally ignore the issues of repairs and replacements and so most of the time, I had been expected to foot the bill from the lower than usual payment rates which had definitely placed me under even more financial pressure.

Financially, the situation had really been

quite difficult to manage and in those days, insurance companies had been very reluctant to cover any potential damages by clients that had been perceived as high risk and unfortunately, local authority clients had generally been deemed and classified as high risk. Despite all the problematic hurdles however, I had found ways to cope and I'd managed to soldier on as I had clambered over some dramatic, chaotic and financial hurdles and had crashed straight into others. Although I hadn't escaped that first year without some heavy debts, emotional scars and psychological wounds due to my ignorance and misfortunate experiences, I had at least tried to accept the harsh realities that I'd faced and had wrapped the bandages formed from experience gently around my head each night.

Much to my absolute horror however, not long after the first difficult year had gone by, things had suddenly taken a turn for the worse when I had been allocated a new guest by Mike Walker, the local authority liaison officer that had dealt with the provision of temporary accommodation for clients and the local suppliers of such accommodation in Camden

Town. Unlike the usual arrival of guests, this particular guest's arrival had totally shocked the living daylights out of me for more reasons than one and nothing about his entrance to the interior of the hotel had been pleasant and to be perfectly frank, it had absolutely horrified me so much that my bones had shaken right down to my toes.

Rather shockingly, much to my absolute horror and total disbelief, the man that had been brought to and allocated the hotel on that particular occasion for actual temporary accommodation had been the man that had taken an actual dump upon the hotel's front doorsteps. When it came to the actual issue of local authority clients, some of them had in fact been homeless prior to their arrival at the hotel and so his homeless status hadn't bothered me in the slightest or been perceived as a problem in itself but his past conduct towards the hotel, the hotel's guests and myself had definitely presented more than one issue to me and none of them had been pleasant. Despite the very negative past history that we had shared however, suddenly this perverse man had turned up on my doorstep in a legitimate manner and I'd had to not only swallow that unpleasantness but I had also had to welcome him into the confines of my hotel and accept his presence inside the hotel's walls for an indefinite time period which I'd truly hoped at the time wouldn't be for too long.

On the actual afternoon of the man's arrival, I had been in the midst of some paperwork inside my room when there had been a knock at the door and since it had sounded official, I'd immediately dropped everything and then jumped up to answer it. Since a visit from the local housing coordinator had been expected that afternoon between a two-hour time slot, the arrival of both the local housing coordinator and the new guest had been expected but the actual identity of the new guest intake had been a total shock to me when I had actually opened up the hotel's front door and then had found the man who had been referred to as Bert stood upon my doorstep.

“Hi Mr. Gethin, I'm Louise one of your local housing coordinators, I work for Mike and this is Bert your new guest." The female coordinator had mentioned as she had politely introduced both herself and the new client.

Due to my state of total shock, a nervous lump had immediately gathered inside my throat as I had attempted to squeeze some words out of my horrified mouth but paralysis had suddenly gripped every inch of my frame and then had held me totally captive as my own words had stuck to my lips and my tongue. The whole moment had been tremendously uncomfortable for me to face and then have to actually accept as I had offered the female coordinator that had brought Bert to the hotel's front door just a very tense smile and strained nod of compliance and then I'd stepped back from the door as I had prepared to allow the two to step inside the premises. According to what I had already known at the time, Mike Walker really hadn't been the kind of man that one could negotiate with because he had usually just snapped and barked instructions at people and so my potential refusal to participate hadn't been a viable option, not if I'd wanted to continue with the agreement that I had made with the local authority and not if I'd wanted to be given a regular stream of clients and so I had participated, extremely reluctantly.

"Please come in." I had finally managed to blurt out as I'd opened up the front door a bit wider.

A nervous tense expression had immediately, rapidly crossed my face as the two had stepped inside the building because although I had been sent Bert's details and a letter to say that he had been due to arrive that day by the local authority prior to their arrival, I hadn't actually known at the time that I'd already met Bert, more than once. Irrespective of my prior disgust when it came to the actual issue of Bert's filthy, past exhibitions however, it appeared that he had been allocated to stay at my actual hotel and although he had been responsible for so much disgusting drama in the past, I had felt utterly powerless to oppose his presence, purely due to my financial reliance upon the local authority and their clients in order to sustain some of the building's essential overheads and to service the debts for repairs to cover the damages that some of their clients had caused.

Some part of me had wondered at the time, if my face had given away my intense disgust and if Louise had been able to sense my hesitation as I had begun to shake my head in total defeat and then had silently started to deliberate over exactly how to respond. For the very first time ever, since I had entered into an agreement with the local authority, I'd suddenly begun to question whether or not I could reject a potential guest that had been allocated to me by Mike Walker and whether I could possibly do so without any fear of future ramifications that might stem from that rejection and my wall of refusal but I had been unable to raise the issue and to seek further clarity on the matter with Louise at that point, due to Bert's actual presence.

From what I had agreed to with the local authority, the agreement had stated that I'd accommodate anyone that they had decided to allocate to the hotel and that had generally been a blanket of acceptance that had applied to all of their clients and from what I had experienced prior to that point in time, there had been no real exclusion clauses. One minor exclusion on my part could perhaps be applied, if there had been some kind of legal issue that had involved some kind of criminal element but that one minor exclusion clause had therefore meant that I had effectively, already agreed to house Bert because when he had committed those filthy acts, I hadn't notified any law enforcements agencies. The previous naked display and past dump on the hotel's doorstep by Bert hadn't been reported to anyone at the time and so, I had felt that it would be highly unlikely that such complaints might be taken seriously after his allocation and arrival and certainly not seriously enough to find him alternative accommodation straight away which had meant that my hands had effectively been tied firmly behind my back purely due to my own past lack of action.

Just a few seconds later as I had walked along the hallway with Louise the housing coordinator and Bert towards the hotel's communal lounge, I'd somehow managed to maintain my balance, even though some parts of me had wanted to collapse in a defeated heap on the ground but as I had walked, I'd bravely prepared to take him to the vacant room that it had already been agreed that he'd stay in, when we had bumped into Ursula en-route. A look of panic stricken horror had immediately crossed Ursula's face, I had observed as I'd glanced into her eyes and then watched in silence as some flickers of fear, tension and shocked recognition had stumbled across every inch of her face and the fearful wince and trembles from her body that had followed, had clearly indicated to me that she had been as mortified as I had been by Bert's sudden appearance inside the hotel as a legitimate client that had needed to be accommodated and actually housed. Despite our combined horror however, I had forced myself to offer Ursula a tense, nervous smile before I'd continued to lead the coordinator and Bert towards the communal guest lounge where upon arrival, I had then left them alone together for a few minutes as I'd returned to my own room and makeshift office to collect the keys for the respective guest room that Bert had been due to occupy.

Once I had retrieved the guest room key from my office and then had returned to the hotel's communal guest lounge, I'd had to show Bert to his actual guest room but as I had walked towards the guest room door, a nervous, horrified lump of discomfort had gathered inside my throat that had made it almost impossible for me to breathe. Suddenly that day, the tides of the financial solution that had saved me throughout that first year from a rapid descent from the clifftops of financial survival had really turned against me and it had presented me with the real ugliness of what I had actually agreed to participate in, had fully signed up for and what I'd accepted to function alongside and there had been no escape hatch to leap out off. No rescues missions it had appeared had been on the way at the time to rescue me and so, I had shown Bert into the guest room and then had reluctantly handed him the room key after which point, the coordinator and I had left him inside the guest room with his small bag of possessions without so much as even a single word of further discussion.

The uncomfortable lump of discomfort in my throat had continued to grow as I had walked back along the hallway towards the hotel front door with the coordinator as I'd begun to accept that no matter what, Bert had to stay for the night and possibly even for the coming week and that nervous, shocked lump of discomfort in my throat would therefore have to be swallowed. Not more than a few minutes later, the coordinator and I had arrived back beside the front door and as I'd prepared to bid her farewell, I had thrown a few questions at her in an attempt to establish if an ejection of Bert in the near future might be actually possible.

Due to the nature of Bert's past appearances, I had harbored absolutely no desire at all to house the man inside my hotel and so I'd worried immensely about what Bert might do next and what impact it might have upon those around him. A huge area of concern for me had revolved around the female guests because I had seen Bert expose himself publicly in the past and had even seen him masturbate on the street in full public view, so I'd feared what might happen inside the hotel's four walls, simply because he had been accommodated inside the building and so, I had expressed some of these concerns directly and verbally to Louise as she had prepared to depart.

"Look Mr. Gethin, I know he might not be the ideal guest and that you have raised some very valid concerns, so I'll speak to Mike about it." Louise had swiftly reassured me. "If you can just tolerate the situation in the meantime though, I might be able to find him somewhere slightly more suitable by next week."

"Thanks." I had replied appreciatively as I'd nodded. "I know that he's been sleeping rough, does he have any money for food and meals?"

"Yes, he's been given some food vouchers and a small loan to help him buy some necessities and his application for benefits has already been submitted." Louise had explained. "So, he should be fine."

Although Louise had given me some reassurances that Bert might not be around for very long and that had comforted me to some extent as she had started to walk away, I had shaken my head in total frustration as I'd watched her depart because I had known that a lot of trouble could happen in a week and that Bert had been a lot of disgusting trouble in the past, in less than a couple of hours. For the remainder of that day and well into the evening my mood had remained miserable as I'd wallowed in my misfortune and absolute dismay and as I had faced some of the other guests throughout that evening, I'd had to face their total shock and utter disbelief too and Cherie of course had been one of the most outspoken and vocal about the issue of Bert, when I had bumped into her in the hallway en-route to the communal kitchen. A brief conversation had rapidly begun about Bert and his presence in the hotel because by that point, Cherie had actually discovered that Bert had been housed inside the premises and although she'd had many questions, unfortunately, I had possessed absolutely none of the actual answers.

"Is he here to stay Mr. Gethin?" Cherie had asked. "Do they know that he masturbates in public?"

"Well Cherie, I have asked for him to be moved as soon as possible but that probably won't happen until at least next week." I had replied. "In the meantime, you should probably just try to stay out of his way."

"That won't be hard, I'll stay as far away from him as I possibly can." Cherie had replied with a grin. "I guess you don't really have much of a choice in who they send here."

"No, I don't and today I found that out because I would not have ever agreed to accommodate him if I had." I had pointed out. "In fact, if it had been up to me, he would not have even stepped foot inside these four walls. So many different kinds of people walk through these doors Cherie and unfortunately, I can't control who they send here or their conduct once they arrive."

"Oh my gosh, I can't imagine what he'll do now that he's actually inside the building." Cherie had teased. "Since he did make such a mess outside of it."

"Hopefully, he won't have time to do very much and he'll be gone soon." I had reassured her. "I've put in a request already."

For the first evening of Bert's stay, quite surprisingly, nothing untoward had actually occurred but as I had relaxed that night and prepared to sleep, I'd definitely worried about and feared what the next morning might bring because I had felt an undercurrent of discomfort run through my veins. Both Cherie and Ursula had been wary of Bert's sudden appearance and rightly so, because technically, he had caused a lot of drama already and as far as I had been concerned, he had been a human package of mucky chaos that had been wrapped in total perversion and absolute filth and Bert's filth couldn't simply be washed away with something as simple as a shower or a bath. In terms of Bert's personal hygiene and the lack of it, due to his homeless status prior to his arrival I had understood that to some extent and had even initially sympathized with his misfortune when he had first appeared at the hotel's front door but the mucky, filthy, perverted public displays, I'd found almost repulsive, totally unacceptable and absolutely inexcusable.

Once the next morning had arrived however, so too had Bert's first perverted incident as quite early in the morning and before I had even woken up properly, several alarm filled shrieks had emanated from the bathroom on the ground floor and so I had grabbed my robe, slippers and room door keys from the peg and then rushed out of my room to investigate the source of the noise. Much to my absolute horror, total disgust and my fearful predictions, I had found a female guest Mildred stuck in the bathroom between the bath and door in a state of total shock and she had looked absolutely horrified as she'd shaken her head at me and then had begun to sob.

"He followed me into the bathroom Mr. Gethin and when I tried to leave, he blocked the door." Mildred had sobbed. "Then he started to take his clothes off."

Every inch of my body had started to shake in anger as I had turned to face Bert and had glanced at his almost naked body but my shaken response had not just been due to anger but also partially, due to my own fear. In terms of Bert's size, he hadn't been a small man and he had actually been a lot taller than me and so I had worried that if things became physical between us, I'd be unable to face that challenge and be unable to overpower him effectively.

"Bert, you need to put your clothes back on

immediately and get the hell out of this bathroom right now." I had demanded.

A pair of soiled tracksuit bottoms had been reluctantly picked up of the floor just a few seconds later as Bert had begun to cooperate with my request but my body had continued to shake as a mixture of fear, outrage and anger had simmered just below the surface of my skin as I had stood on guard by the bathroom door and had kept a watchful eye upon him. Just a few seconds later I had given Mildred, who had been a mild-mannered woman in her late fifties, a nod of reassurance and so she had rapidly picked up her belongings from the side of the bath, wrapped them safely up inside her robe and had then tucked her robe under her arm just before she had fled the interior of the bathroom as she'd left me totally alone with Bert. Not a single word had been spoken by Bert as he had continued to dress himself and then as he'd walked towards the bathroom door and towards me, I had noticed that not even a single apology had been offered for his conduct to either Mildred or myself.

"You are now on an official warning Bert." I

had warned him sternly. "If there's another incident like this one, you're out of here and you won't be coming back."

Some part of me deep down inside had wanted to turf Bert out on his backside straight away but due to the agreement that I had made, I'd known at the time that such actions on my part would only create more problems for me in the long run and so I had to bide my time and hope that they would move him soon or that he'd do something else that would allow me to eject from the premises immediately. A complaint however, had been an option at my disposal and so as I had waited for Bert to fully vacate the room, I'd thoughtfully begun to consider how I would complain and who I'd complain too as I had retained my still but angry silence.

For a few brief seconds Bert had actually paused when he had arrived at the door and my position and as he'd given me a spiteful stare laced with utter hate and total contempt, I must admit for that few brief seconds, I had feared what might happen next between us both. When it had come to the issue of fist fights, I hadn't been built particularly well and so in school yard brawls, throughout my younger years, I had always come off the worst and so any such fights had always been an easy win for the far stronger lads. However, I had plastered an angry scowl across my face as I'd stared angrily back at Bert as I had made a brave attempt to stand up for myself and to stand up to him.

After Bert had visually sized me up a bit and a few more seconds had passed by, he had then left the bathroom and not even a single word had been released from his lips as he'd gone and so as the bathroom had emptied, I had released a sigh of total relief as I'd watched his soiled tail vanish from sight without any further drama. Since it had been the weekend and a Saturday morning, I had worried that I would not be able to reach the local housing coordinator with a phone call and a verbal complaint which I'd definitely felt at the time had been extremely crucial because Bert's conduct I had predicted, could and would only get worse and I'd doubted my ability to physically challenge him, if and when that negative downward spiral actually happened.

Approximately one hour later, once I had returned to my makeshift office with Mildred in tow who I'd asked to provide me with a precise verbal account of Bert's actions, I had offered her a seat and then sat down beside my desk as I'd prepared to write down the details of the incident. For the next fifteen minutes or so, I had listened to Mildred speak and as she had related every minute detail to me, I'd shuddered in total disgust because it really had been such a traumatic and scary experience for her. When it had come to the actual issue of Bert himself as I had scribbled down some notes and had continued to listen to Mildred speak, there had not been a shadow of a doubt inside my mind that he had been a total and utter creep and not even a bath, a warm bed, a roof over his head, access to a kitchen and some money in his pocket had been able to change his filthy nature or his despicable, perverse behavior.

From that point on I had started to keep a much closer, far more watchful eye on Bert as the weekend had progressed but when the Saturday night had arrived, due to my own physical requirements, my body had still required rest and so it hadn't been possible to watch his every movement or breath but I'd prepared to rest that night in a very wary state indeed. In a single day Bert had stepped into the interior of my life and into the interior of my hotel and he had no longer been just an external threat that could be avoided to some extent by a closed front door because he had been situated inside the building and so that front door had no longer been an viable shield and if anything, the hotel's front door had instead, suddenly become the enabler that had welcomed him into the interior of the building.

My whole perspective on Bert had suddenly been forced to shift from one of total avoidance and contempt to an uncomfortable, tense tolerance but in the midst of that forced tolerance, I had known that I'd still had a duty to protect the other guests from Bert's presence and his conduct towards them, even though the sudden shift in dynamics had totally shocked and absolutely horrified me. Due to a strange twist of fate, Bert had no longer been an external threat and a remote nuisance and virtually, in the blink of an eye, he had become an internal threat and an unavoidable pest that had occupied an actual guest room inside my hotel and inside my actual home.

Throughout that Saturday night as the weekend had progressed, I had tossed and turned practically all night as I'd been haunted by nightmares that had predominantly revolved around what Bert might do whilst in residence at the hotel because I had feared the future and any negative manifestations of his perverse behavior that may occur. A deep uncertainty had lain inside my mind since Bert's arrival and even more so after the bathroom incident with Mildred as to how his conduct might be towards some of the other guests because he had been so unpredictable and I had not known his capabilities or his limits and his past perverted displays had been a huge concern to me and so, I had worried about the possibility of violent outbursts, sexual violence and even more perverted displays. Quite suddenly and very unexpectedly, this strange, awful, perverse man that had seemed to be a garbage bag filled with perversion, junk and filth had stepped into my personal space and life and I'd had to not only accept him but also accommodate him in the same building where I had lived myself and had lain my head and that shift in dynamics coupled with the forced, uncomfortable, tense tolerance that I'd had to extend towards him, to be perfectly frank had absolutely horrified me.

Fortunately, however, the Saturday night had gone by quietly and peacefully enough but by the time the Sunday morning had arrived, so too had more of Bert's drama as I had heard a loud thud come from the communal guest lounge and had then leapt out of bed to respond to the shrieks that had accompanied that very loud thud. Just a few seconds later, once I had grabbed my robe and my set of keys from the hook and then darted out of my room, I'd rushed towards the communal lounge area where I had found Cherie and Bert in the midst of a very heated argument. Apparently and much to my total horror, it had rapidly transpired that Bert had not only been inside the communal kitchen when Cherie had arrived to cook breakfast for her husband and herself that morning as usual but that he had also been partially naked and then he had blocked her facilitation of the cooker and had even flashed some of his private body parts at her.

"Really Mr. Gethin, this man is disgusting." Cherie had complained. "And I've already told him that no one wants to see his scrappy, little bits but he keeps putting them on display."

Due to the all the commotion, Noel had then stridden into the communal guest kitchen just a few seconds later and as he had glanced at Bert and Cherie's upset state, he had angrily shaken his head and then had begun to roll up his sleeves.

"Noel, he flashed his tiny bits at me." Cherie had explained.

A look of total thunder had rapidly crossed Noel's face as he had stepped towards Bert and so I had quickly responded as I'd tried to step in and calm Noel down.

"Noel please don't." I had pleaded as I'd placed my arm on his. "He's really not worth it."

"Don't you ever dare disrespect my wife ever again." Noel had snapped as he had shaken his head and pointed an angry finger at Bert. "Because I don't have to tolerate you or your filth and I won't and if you keep showing people what you don't have, someone will cut off that tiny thing you do have."

"Bert, you're out of here first thing Monday morning." I had insisted as I'd turned to face him.

Several other guests by this point had gathered inside the hallway just outside the communal lounge and kitchen area and a couple had even stepped into the adjoined lounge and so, once I had angrily shaken my head at Bert once more, I had then gently held onto Noel's arm and had begun to lead him towards the hallway as I'd silently guided him away from Bert, the kitchen and the source of his anger. Much to my satisfaction, just a few seconds later Bert had suddenly grabbed his dirty, soiled tracksuit bottoms and then had fled form the communal guest kitchen and a sigh of relief had escaped from my lips as he had rushed out of the room and then along the hallway as I had watched him depart.

"Don't worry Noel, he'll be out of here on Monday morning." I had reassured him.

"Either he goes or we go." Noel had

replied. "I can't have a man behaving like that towards my wife every time she has to step out of our room to cook us a meal."

"He'll be going." I had reiterated. "They have to move him straight away that is the second act of indecent exposure in just one weekend."

"Come on Cherie, we'll eat breakfast out today." Noel had insisted as he had gently taken her arm.

Every part of me had seethed with anger as I had watched Noel and Cherie depart because I'd been absolutely horrified by Bert's actions once again and as I had also known at the time, if I hadn't been present in all likelihood Noel would have physically demolished him. One small glimmer of comfort had accompanied me however, as I had begun to make my way back towards my room and my small office area to make some complaint notes about the second incident and that had been the fact that both incidents collectively had definitely been enough of a justification to eject Bert from the premises in a truly legitimate manner and to hammer the final nail into his coffin of perversion.

When the Monday morning had arrived, fortunately and thankfully, I had been able to reach Louse by phone quite easily and she had immediately agreed to attend the premises by lunchtime. Once Louise had arrived, I had immediately shown her into my office and had then offered her a seat as I'd prepared to enlighten her as to Bert's conduct since his arrival and to show her the complaint notes that had been made since her last visit. Deep down inside my body however, I had felt my nerves rattle around as I'd taken a deep breath, sat down opposite her and then had begun to fidget with some pens and pieces of paper because technically, as I had already known at the time, my position had not really been one of great strength. Due to my financial reliance upon local authority clients, I had pretty much been at the mercy of the liaison officer that had been allocated to the hotel by the local authority itself and as I'd already known, Mike Walker hadn't been the kind of person that one would want to argue with because he had been well known for his tough attitude but nonetheless, I had prepared to negotiate in an attempt to define my own terms of acceptability.

"Look Louise, I appreciate that you haven't really had much time to find Bert alternative accommodation but I have to be frank, he can't stay here any longer." I had finally blurted out as I'd glanced her face and had shaken my head. "The other guests are scared of him, especially the female guests, he really frightens them. His behavior is on par with a sexual predator and so, they are very scared of him. Since Friday, he has indecently exposed himself to two female guests and one he actually trapped inside a bathroom during the incident. If you don't get him off the premises today, I'll have to ask the women if they want me to call the police and if they wish to press charges against him."

The next few minutes had been spent in a deep discussion as I had related every single detail of each incident to Louise and had insisted that Bert really could not stay in the Happyvale Hotel for even an hour longer. Although I hadn't had much of a choice when it had come to the issue of the local authority and who they had decided to send to the hotel that morning, I had been absolutely adamant that there had to be some kind of limits and that if my hotel had to be the dumping ground of the borough, I'd have to at least have some choice in the matter, especially when it came to the provision of accommodation to people like Bert and Pervy Pete. Some of the terms of my agreement with the local authority had to be defined and translated on my terms to some extent and so that morning I had started to stand up for myself in some ways because I'd realized at that point that if I had failed to do so that day, I would be totally bulldozed over by Mike Walker and ground into the ground from that point onwards.

Much to my total relief, Louise hadn't kicked up a fuss and once she had listened to all the complaints in full, she had then begun to nod her head and had finally agreed to remove Bert from the premises immediately. Approximately thirty minutes later, once I had notified Bert of Louise's decision and he had collected his small bag of personal items, I'd watched in joyful silence as Bert had vacated the premises and as Louise had led him away, I had rejoiced in my victory that day because his ejection from the premises had not only been swift but also painless. Although it had been a small step that I had taken that day that small step had been a hugely important one for me because it had clarified to Mike Walker that even though he might have considered the Happyvale Hotel to be one of the worst hotel's in London that even the worst had their own limits and levels of decency and that sexual predators and perverts had not been welcome or acceptable in my hotel.

DRUGS, SEX, RATS AND ALCOHOL

Fortunately for my mother, she had not been alive to see the hotel under my management because she would have been absolutely horrified by the results which had been really awful, especially for me as the proprietor since the responsibility for the mess that had lain at my door and upon my pillow each night. Unfortunately, the very heavy responsibilities that management of the Happyvale Hotel had entailed couldn't be given to anyone else because the delegation of the troubles that I had faced hadn't been an option at the time, since there had been no one else to take responsibility for the mess but me. Generally, as the second year of my hotel ownership had been ushered in, things had continued on a downwards spiral and had even become far worse as I had continued to run the establishment the best I could which it had quickly become apparent, really hadn't been good enough because the legal issues that I'd faced had lain far outside the scope of my knowledge.

For the most part, the knotted entanglement of legal issues that had arisen and that had tied their knots firmly around the hotel's four walls had only become worse after the first year and had put the establishment and me fully at the mercy of other people's decisions. The hotel's interior had been filled up time and time again with predominantly, antisocial guests that no one else in Camden had wanted to accept or house in any capacity and so, I had fallen deeper and deeper into a pit of despair with my body and mind tightly strapped up by the ropes of legal complexities that had bound my every limb and rendered me, totally and absolutely powerless.

Sadly, by the end of the first few months in the second year, antisocial behavior had become an everyday occurrence and acts of prostitution had been conducted regularly upon the hotel's front doorstep and even inside the hotel itself. A stream of drugs had flowed through the bricks of the building as frequently as the cockroaches and rats had scurried around under the floorboards and so all my good intentions had virtually collapsed, since not only had there been an abundance of illegal substances but also the rats had returned and their number seemed to have actually increased.

Some of the guests had expressed their fears to me about the cockroach infestation and rat invasion because they had felt reluctant to shower and bath, just in case a rat had jumped out and bit them as they did so but I had lacked the financial means to really clean the building out again from top to bottom since I'd been knee deep in debt. In some ways, it had almost felt as if the hotel had been visited by the biblical plagues, albeit a much milder version and so I had remained fearful to see how and if the rest of those plagues would present themselves inside the hotel's four walls as the second year had continued. Due to the general lack of hygiene inside the building itself and the run-down state of the hotel's facilities by that point, any efforts to fumigate the premises as I had already known, would barely have even scratched the surface of those problems and so to some extent, a few months into that second year, I'd almost given up on my efforts to try and make the Happyvale Hotel a decent place to stay.

When it had come to the actual issue of the hotel's interior, every part of it by that point had looked run down, limp and lifeless and there had been no real hope of resuscitation because I had been unable to make any major cosmetic changes to its general state due to the financial difficulties that I'd faced. Every single inch of the hotel had suffered from the lack of hygienic respect shown to it by the majority of the guests and from the skeleton of maintenance that I had been able to afford from my strained finances and so, the downward spiral had continued as the second year had continued and I'd tried to soldier on as I had held the bones of the hotel's almost lifeless corpse together and wished for some kind of life support machine to help me resuscitate its heart. Decent standards of cleanliness had totally slipped into a very filthy norm and as I had realized at the time, Ursula had been locked in a battle that she could never even possibly hope to win because hardly any of the guests ever bothered to clean up after themselves and the adjoined communal kitchen and lounge had become a total state along with the halls and the communal bathrooms.

Although I hadn't wanted things to deteriorate and although I had sought to try and keep basic standards of decency in place, the drugs and alcoholic outbursts had decorated the interior of the hotel's four walls in a nasty, murky tone every single day and so I'd really struggled to instill and maintain any kind of order. Several of the guests that had arrived in the early part of that second year, I had rapidly discovered, had been heavily involved with local drug dealers and due to their associations, I'd often faced violent outbursts inside the hotel itself which had revolved around disagreements with other guests about drugs and money and those disagreements had occurred quite regularly and definitely more than just once a week.

One such guest had been Jonas who had been a local authority client intake that had arrived in the first month in the second year and at first, he had seemed quite usual in that he'd arrived with the local housing coordinator and his small bag of possessions. Upon Jonas's arrival it had been agreed that he would be housed at the hotel for approximately six months and so, I had quickly settled him and had then shown him around in as had been usual practice with local authority clients. Quite unusually however, Jonas had seemed to gravitate towards and then had formed a close association with another male guest called Vernon who most other guests had avoided, since Vernon had been very much like the Italian Thief Mario, who had since been rehoused, in that he had been a thief to the core with very light fingers.

Due to changes in guest occupancy, thankfully and fortunately for me, Mario the Italian Thief had no longer been in occupation at the time since both he and his wife had been rehoused along with Pervy Pete, much to my total relief but as the hotel's interior had transcended into even more dramatic chaos, at times I had even wished for the Mario's return. Since I had already decided to venture into the local authority's client base and had fully dove into that customer base, I'd had to almost accept anyone and everyone that Mike Walker had decided to throw at the hotel's front door but as I had begun to realize by that point, the departure of one problematic local authority client had usually only meant one thing for me, the arrival of another human headache and there had been very few exceptions to that general downward spiral in client base.

In what had seemed like no time at all, Vernon and Jonas had cemented their friendship, tapped into the local drug suppliers, joined an underground fence ring for stolen goods and the duo had even started to dabble in prostitution rackets and so my hotel as a result had rapidly descended into even more of a pigsty and had transcended into an absolute cesspit of total vice. All of sudden, Pervy Pete and Mario the Italian Thief had almost looked like a cup of tea because this hardcore crime duo had been far more organized, a lot more calculated and combined, a total nightmare from start to finish that had felt more like a hard whiskey on the rocks.

Throughout that first six months of that second year, my life and the hotel's interior had become increasingly complicated because during that time I'd had to cope with not only the daily violent outbursts, drug induced arguments between guests, regular thievery from some of the guest rooms, the rat and cockroach infestations but also on top of all that the gruesome twosome, Vernon and Jonas. The two men Vernon and Jonas had kept their activities predominantly outside the hotel premises for the most part and due to the external nature of those activities, it had been hard to challenge them about anything and difficult to catch them red handed because they had rarely conducted those activities visibly on the premises however, they'd involved many of the local authority guests that had been in residence at the time. From the information that I had been given by some of the other guests, I'd known that they had regularly served as go betweens for the local drug dealers, intermediaries for a stolen goods fence ring and even as some kind of pimps for a local prostitution racket and that they'd recruited some of the actual participants in those crime rackets from the hotel itself.

More than one or two people had been persuaded to participate in the stolen goods fence ring and from what I had heard, the two men had even sent a few of the hotel's guests out on thievery trips from local shops and to steal from people that they had targeted in the local area that they'd deemed to be wealthy. Since the majority of the proceeds from such thefts and the prostitution had ended up expended on drug deals that the two men had also been active participants in and had organized, they had managed to take a slice of income from not only the fence of the stolen goods but also from the proceeds that the individual responsible had then later spent on drugs and so they'd cut a slice of profit from both sides and from both crimes. Essentially, they had found an easy way to profit from some of the hotel's occupants, most of whom had been local authority clients like themselves and many of whom had been hard up and financially desperate and that had even extended at times, to actual involvement in prostitution.

One such female resident that had been involved with the two men had been called Cathy and she had broken down in tears one Saturday afternoon when I had found her outside in the back garden in a drunken, drugged up state and then had listened to her speak as she'd finally confided in me. Due to the debts that Cathy had owed to the two men, who had given her a supply of drugs to feed her drug habit, she had owed them quite a lot of money and so the two men had basically rented her out as a hooker until she'd cleared the debts that she had owed them. Unfortunately, since Cathy had continued to take drugs however, that debt had never actually reduced and if anything, it had actually grown larger and larger and so after a few months, she had almost collapsed one day at the hotel, due to the pressure from the two men and the prostitution that she'd had to engage in, in order to satisfy those debts.

"I just don't know what to do Mr. Gethin." Cathy had sobbed. "If I don't pay them the money that I owe them, they'll probably beat me up."

"Maybe you should leave the hotel." I had suggested as I'd sat down beside her amongst the weeds upon a tree stump. "I could always ask them to move you."

"What if I leave and then they come and look for me?" Cathy had asked as she had faced me and then shaken her head. "They might actually find me and then they'll be even more angry because I tried to run away from them."

"You need to get some help Cathy." I had advised. "If you keep buying drugs from them, the debts will only get bigger."

"I know Mr. Gethin but it's so hard to stop, it calls to you and your body needs it, it's like a hunger that nothing else can satisfy. When you don't have it you feel angry, sad and depressed and at times, you can even feel this pain inside of you and you walk around like a zombie." Cathy had explained. "Then when you take it again, it soothes all the pain and it keeps you calm, so that you can face life again and the people in it."

"But that's not real Cathy because before

you were on drugs, you didn't need anything like that to face life." I had tried to convince her. "The withdrawal from the drugs is what makes you feel depressed, sad, weak and angry, the withdrawal makes you think that you need it to live and to cope with life."

"It's very hard for me Mr. Gethin, cocaine is a very powerful drug." Cathy had admitted. "You can't just walk away from it, or ignore it, it calls to you and it finds you wherever you go. You can try and try and try to walk away from it but people who know, they can see it in your eyes and they will tempt you and one day, you'll be weak and you will want that high again that you miss so much because you'll need to satisfy that urge that runs through your veins, it makes you feel so powerful, it makes feel like you can do anything and that you can face anyone, it makes you feel so strong. Once you take cocaine, you can never get away from it, never ever, you can't divorce cocaine or get an injunction against it, it's everywhere you go, on every street corner and in every drug dealer's eyes and face and everywhere you go, it waits for you, it waits for you to be weak."

"I guess it's really hard for me to understand Cathy, it's not something that I've ever experienced." I had concluded. "Can't you get help from a rehabilitation center or something? Don't they have programs to help people?"

"I can't afford fancy treatment centers and if you try to get help from the government funded drug rehabilitation centers, you're then labelled as a drug addict and life becomes even more difficult." Cathy had explained. "You can't get a job, you can't do anything."

"What about if you told people about them and about the drugs and the prostitution?" I had ventured to ask. "They probably have a few women like you Cathy, they're probably doing the same thing to other women."

"They would want to kill me Mr. Gethin and so would their dealers." Cathy had replied. "And then I wouldn't be safe anywhere I went, they'd be looking for me and their people would be looking for me."

"Will it help if I ask the housing department to move you?" I had asked.

"Perhaps that might help a bit." Cathy had acknowledged. "Then the drugs wouldn't be so easy to get because I wouldn't be around them. The housing would want to know though, why I need to be moved. I doubt they'd move me for no reason."

"I know." I had agreed. "Leave it with me for a few days Cathy and I'll try to come up with something."

Every part of me had sympathized with Cathy's position as I had left her side and had returned to my lounge but my hands had literally been tied because without a direct confrontation which as I'd already known at the time had been likely to take a violent turn, I had been powerless to assist. A few other possible solutions had been considered but all of those potential solutions as I had already known, had required the cooperation of Mike Walker and since he hadn't generally been a helpful person that had understood the baggage of complexities that local authority clients had often brought along with them, I had felt it highly unlikely that he'd participate and offer to provide either Cathy or myself with a suitable solution.

For the next few days I had pondered over Cathy's dilemma as I'd coped with the usual daily drama of the hotel but by the Thursday evening, things had taken a hard nose dive into the deep end of trouble as Cherie had suddenly banged on my door at around eight that evening and had demanded my immediate attention. Since I had just eaten my evening meal and I'd even begun to relax with my usual bottle of wine and the radio program that I had listened to most evenings, initially I'd been in a much more relaxed state than usual but Cherie's shrieks had demanded and required an alert, instant reaction and so I had begun to respond as I'd grabbed my shoes, the room keys from the key hook by the door and then had opened up my door.

"You have to come now Mr. Gethin." Cherie had shrieked. "It's Cathy."

"Where is she?" I had asked as I'd stepped out into the hallway.

"She's outside, at the end of the street." Cherie had explained. "And she is in a very bad way."

"Okay, I'm coming now Cherie." I had replied as I'd quickly pulled the door shut behind me and then started to walk along the hallway towards the front door.

Just a few seconds later, once we had both vacated the building, I had started to follow Cherie towards the other end of the street as the duskiness of the evening had been ushered in all around me, along with a cold, windy breeze that had whipped and whirled around the street, buildings, parked cars and my body as I'd walked. When we had reached the other end of the street and then had crossed the road, I had found Cathy in a battered, bruised state, hidden between a car and a fence in a crouched ball and she had seemed unable to speak and unable to stand and as I'd just stood and stared at her black and blue face, every part of my body had begun to shake with absolute horror.

"Cherie, I need to call an ambulance immediately." I had insisted as I'd taken off my jacket, knelt down beside Cathy and then placed my coat over her. "You need to stay here with Cathy, I'll be back soon."

"Okay Mr. Gethin." Cherie had swiftly replied. "Can you tell Noel where I am please and ask him to come? I had just popped out to the shops to buy something, so by now, he'll probably be worried."

"Yeah, I'll do that." I had reassured her.

"Will Cathy be alright Mr. Gethin?" Cherie had asked.

For a few seconds I had hesitated as I'd glanced at Cherie's face, her forehead looked crumpled due to all the lines of stressful worry that had gathered there, her eyes looked dim with fear and her voice unlike its usual chirpy tone had sounded broken and warped, cracked by the pure stress and tension that she had so obviously felt.

"I'm not sure Cherie but the sooner I call the ambulance, the more likely it is that she will be." I had convinced her.

"Right." Cherie had agreed.

A horrified, dismayed sigh had been released from my lips as I had given Cathy one last glance and then had rushed off back towards the hotel because as I'd already known at the time, she had looked unconscious and so an ambulance definitely had to be called. Much to my relief, Cherie had agreed to stay by Cathy's side and so once I had returned to my room, I'd made the urgent call and then had quickly left my room again as I had prepared to return to the street corner that Cherie had found Cathy in. Before I had vacated the interior of the hotel for the second time however, I'd quickly called out to Noel from the hallway a few times and within a few minutes, he had not only appeared but had also agreed to accompany me.

Approximately ten minutes later the ambulance had arrived and as I had watched the medical responders start to assist, they had checked Cathy's vital statistics, given her some oxygen, placed a neck brace around her neck and then rolled her onto a stretcher, all within a matter of minutes. Since no one had wanted to get in the way of the medical professionals, Noel, Cherie and myself had stood next to the fence just a few steps away from Cathy's position as we had watched in shocked silence but when one of the medical responders had asked us for Cathy's name, Cherie had verbally responded to her question. Besides that, one very brief conversation however, no one else had uttered even a single word but as the ambulance crew prepared to depart with Cathy, I had drawn much closer to their vehicle and a female medical responder as I'd prepared to ask her a few questions.

"Where will you be taking Cathy?" I had asked her.

"To UCH." The woman had replied.

"Will she be okay?" I had enquired.

"She's in a pretty bad state, it looks like she's been kicked in the face and stomach multiple times, beaten with some kind of object and we think she was hit on the back with some kind of heavy, metal tool." She had explained. "She can't even breathe properly at the moment. Are you her friends?"

"Well, she stays at my hotel, she's in temporary accommodation at the moment." I had replied.

"Can we come to the hospital and see her?" Cherie had asked.

"You should probably come and see her tomorrow, I'd give the doctors a chance to attend to her first." She had advised. "Unless you're a family member or partner, you're only really allowed to see people during the usual hospital visiting hours."

Once the ambulance had left, I had led Cherie and Noel back towards the hotel and we had discussed Cathy's state as we'd walked but we had verbally stumbled as we'd talked due to our horrified shock and the condition that we had found Cathy in. Sadly, I had concluded, as we had arrived back outside the hotel's front door and I had glanced up at the words 'Happyvale Hotel' in bold dark blue letters above the entrance, the reality of the hotel had been situated a million miles away from happiness and Cathy's condition had shown me that day, the very grim reality of what my hotel had really, truly become. In so many ways, I had failed as a hotel owner and Cathy's state had reinforced that failure because my attention had been fully drawn to it that evening and so I'd had to accept that all my hotel had become had been a down trodden cesspit of vice and a haven for crack dealers and pimps, held together by a bit of cracked cement and some worn out bricks.

The next day in the late afternoon I had visited Cathy at the hospital along with Cherie and Noel where we had found Cathy in a hospital ward, lain upon a bed, still in a bruised and battered state and with a drawn, pale face but at least by that point, she had regained consciousness. Several bandages had been wrapped around various parts of Cathy's body and various pieces of medical equipment sat beside her hospital bed and as I had watched Cherie put the bunch of flowers that she had brought along with her in some water and a vase, I'd observed the scene in absolute horror because I had felt that it could have been avoided, if Mike Walker had not just dumped hardened, petty criminals like Vernon and Jonas at my hotel.

"Are you okay Cathy?" Cherie had asked.

"Not really Cherie but apparently, I should recover in a couple of months." Cathy had replied weakly as she had smiled. "Thanks for the flowers."

"Who did this to you Cathy?" Cherie had asked as she had sat down beside her bed and then held her hand.

For a few minutes there had been nothing but silence as I had glanced at Cathy's face and had just tried to read her thoughts because so many questions had lurked inside my mind and I'd really wanted to know if either Vernon or Jonas had been responsible for the physical battery that had taken place. If either of the two men had been responsible, I had vowed at that moment that I would throw them out immediately and even call the police myself and so I'd been anxious to hear Cathy's response.

"It was just some guy." Cathy had replied. "He got angry because I didn't want to do something that he wanted me to do."

"Do you know him?" Cherie asked.

"Did someone from the hotel do this to you Cathy?" I had asked. "If they did you need to tell me right now, so that I can deal with it officially."

"Not really, he was just a punter." Cathy had explained. "He wanted me to do something really perverse and I refused."

"Don't you ever go anywhere near him ever again." Cherie had advised. "You really don't have to do things that you don't want to Cathy, remember that."

Cathy had nodded.

Approximately one hour later, Cherie, Noel and I had left Cathy's bedside and as we had vacated the hospital some discussion had taken place as to Cathy's health and when she might return to the hotel. Since I had been asked by the local authority to keep a room reserved for her, it had been likely that upon her release from hospital that she'd return to the premises but I'd feared for her safety because Jonas and Vernon as I had already known in all likelihood would still be around too. When we had arrived back at the hotel, I had entered into the hallway with Cherie and Noel and just as we had been about to separate, Jonas had stridden into the hallway with a pretentiously concerned expression on his face.

"Oh, did you go and see Cathy?" Jonas had asked. "How was she?"

"What do you care?" I had replied.

Upon Cherie and Noel's faces there had been confused expressions as they had glanced at my face in total bewilderment which had not surprised me because they hadn't known at the time the things that I had known about Jonas and especially when it came to Cathy's situation.

"Look, I just want to know if she's okay." Jonas had insisted. "What's the harm in that?"

"Why, do you need her to buy some more drugs from you, or do you have another punter lined up to pay for the drugs that she buys from you?" I had snapped.

"No, I'm just asking about her health Mr. Gethin. I'm being a friend that's all." Jonas had said as he'd attempted to justify his interest in her.

"A friend to Cathy that's the last thing on

Earth that you are or that you will ever be." I had scorned as I'd shaken my head in anger. "For all I know, you might even be the one that put her in hospital in the first place. She did owe you money for drugs, right?"

"I didn't touch her." Jonas had barked. "And if you keep throwing wild accusations at me, you better get ready to prove them."

Nothing but total silence had filled the hallway for a few seconds before Jonas had stormed off and headed towards his room and just a few minutes later, I had heard a door slam shut. A nervous silence had continued to occupy the hallway for a few more seconds as Cherie and Noel had just stood rooted to the spot in shock as they had shaken their heads but that silence had rapidly been totally trashed as suddenly, a series of very loud thumps had emanated from the first floor and Jonas's room.

"What's he doing Mr. Gethin?" Cherie had asked. "It sounds like he's smashing his room up."

"He probably is, you guys better come in here." I had replied as I'd walked towards my room door and then opened it up. "Just until he calms down."

"Right Mr. Gethin." Noel had agreed.

In a matter of just seconds I had opened up my room door and then had invited the married couple inside as we had all sought refuge and shelter from Jonas's angry outburst and once inside my room, I had rapidly offered them both a seat on the small sofa that sat inside the lounge area. Just a few minutes later the thuds had finally stopped and everything had gone quiet for a few minutes and as we had all glanced at each other's faces, I had hoped that Jonas's angry outburst had come to an actual end.

"Do you think he's finished Mr. Gethin?" Cherie had asked.

No sooner had I opened my mouth to answer Cherie's question however, then Jonas had answered it for me as we had heard a very loud crash come from the ground floor and the communal lounge and kitchen area. Since I had been very worried for our safety at the time, I'd rapidly rushed over to my desk and had then picked up the phone as I had prepared to call the police because I'd feared that Jonas might even kick down my own room door.

"I better call the police Cherie." I had said as I'd shaken my head. "He's definitely not finished yet."

Every inch of my body had trembled as I had picked up the phone and had then called the police and as I'd waited for them to answer my call, I had feared what Jonas might do next because the internal doors of the hotel hadn't been that strong and had definitely been penetrable with a bit of muscle, some hard knocks and a few strong kicks.

"Hello yes, I have a problem with a violent guest that I suspect might be on drugs." I had swiftly explained as soon as my call had been answered. "I need someone to come around right away before he smashes the whole place up and there are other guests in the hotel, so he could injure any one of them."

Fortunately, not more than five minutes had passed by before the police had shown up at the hotel's front door with a van that had at least five officers inside it and once they had entered into the premises, they'd rushed towards the communal lounge and kitchen. Due to Jonas's angry state, it had taken at least three officers to finally pin him down and as they had led him out in handcuffs just a few minutes later, I had sighed with total relief as I'd watched them put Jonas inside their van.

"Can I give you his personal belongings please?" I had asked one of the officers. "He can't possibly come back here."

"Okay, we'll take his belongings with us." The male officer had replied with a nod. "Where's his room?"

"It's on the first floor, I'll just get the spare key." I had said as I'd sighed with relief.

Once I had returned to my room, I'd rapidly collected the spare key, some plastic bags and had quickly notified Cherie and Noel that the coast had been clear, so that they could return to their room and carry on with the rest of their day. A few relieved smiles and nods had been exchanged between the three of us as Cherie and Noel had vacated my room and I had also left with them as I'd returned to the hallway and the police officer, equipped with the spare key and the empty plastic bags. For the next ten minutes I had spent some time in Jonas's room with the police officer as I'd bagged up his personal belongings but I had been shocked by the amount of stolen property that had poked out of the small wooden chest of drawers inside the room because each drawer had been stuffed and packed full of stolen jewelry, electrical goods, aftershaves and perfumes.

"It looks like violence and drugs aren't the only problems you have with this guest." The male police officer had mentioned as he'd started to help.

"Yeah you name it, Jonas did it along with his friend Vernon." I had replied as I'd nodded. "Drugs, prostitution and thievery, he had a hand and a foot in every criminal pie that he could dip himself into. I'll just be glad to get rid of him."

"Well, we can only do him for criminal damage today, unless we can get some identification on the stolen property." The police officer had explained.

"That'll be good enough for me, it'll keep him out of my hotel and away from my front door." I had reassured him. "Now, I just have to find a way to get rid of his partner in crime Vernon, I doubt the housing will move him without a fuss."

"Look Mr. Gethin if you want, I can put in a recommendation that will ensure that neither of the two men should be rehoused in central Camden, if that'll help?" He had offered as he'd paused for a moment and had turned to face me.

"It sure will." I had immediately agreed. "Thanks so much, they've been a total nightmare from start to finish."

"No problem. I see people like Jonas every day, small time crooks with big time criminal ambitions." He had reassured me.

"Do you think I'll need an injunction to keep them both away from the premises?" I had asked. "It's just that there are female guests here and so I'm worried that their lifestyle might put some of their lives in danger."

"I wouldn't bother unless they return." He had advised. "Usually petty criminals just move on and find another area to operate in, once they've been kicked out of one and officially warned away. They don't like all the legal attention, especially if they are involved in drugs and so normally, they try to avoid a legal fuss and court rooms if they can."

"What if someone at the hotel owes them money?" I had asked. "They might try to come back to collect it."

"Don't worry Mr. Gethin, if you give me Vernon's details, I'll get him moved too and I'll warn them both to stay away." The police officer had rapidly replied. "I doubt they'll come back."

True to the officer's word by Monday lunchtime there had been an actual visit from a housing coordinator and Vernon had been moved to alternative temporary accommodation and so I had appreciated his efforts and prompt action which had ejected the duo of trouble from the premises in one weekend. A few weeks later Cathy had returned to the hotel but only for a few hours because she hadn't planned to stay for long as I had rapidly discovered upon her return. Due to Cathy's hospitalization Cherie and Noel had gathered in the communal lounge to greet her as the cab had dropped her off outside the building at around lunchtime on the Monday morning of that week and then I had helped her inside with some small bags of personal belongings and as we had made our way towards the communal lounge, she had started to tell me about her plans for the immediate future.

"I've decided Mr. Gethin to take your advice." Cathy had explained.

"You have Cathy?" I had asked as I'd stepped into the lounge.

"Yes, I've booked myself into a woman's treatment center and I'm going to change my life. Apparently, at this treatment center, they help you get clean and help you to find a decent job." Cathy had explained. "A few months from now, you won't even recognize me."

"I'm really happy for you Cathy." I had

replied. "You need that change."

"Yes, I really do." Cathy had agreed.

For the next hour or so Cherie, Noel and I had spent some time in the communal lounge and kitchen area with Cathy because I'd given Cherie some money earlier that morning to buy some food so that she could prepare a welcome back lunch for Cathy and so, she had cooked up a hearty meal for us all to eat. Once the lunch which had consisted of some steak, potatoes and veg had been consumed, Cherie had then accompanied Cathy to her room to help her pack up her belongings and I had returned to my office area to get on with some paperback but part of me had felt really quite sad as I'd internally begun to prepare myself for Cathy's departure.

An hour or so later, Cherie, Noel and myself had all gathered at the front of the building as the car from the woman's treatment had arrived with a staff member to escort Cathy to the premises and to assist her. For a few minutes, Cherie, Noel and I had stood outside the hotel's front door as we had hugged Cathy and had bid her farewell and as

Cathy had prepared to depart, she had turned to me and then had thanked me for my assistance.

"Thanks Mr. Gethin." Cathy had said. "You really told me some things that I really needed to hear."

"Don't worry about it Cathy, you just sort yourself out okay." I had replied.

"Yeah I will, I promise." Cathy had agreed.

"Please Cathy, do it for you. I don't want to see you in that state again." Cherie had encouraged. "That lifestyle is so risky, so horrible and so full of hurt and pain, you should deserve more out of life than that."

"I know Cherie and thanks so much for everything." Cathy had said as she had given her a final affectionate hug. "I better get moving."

"Take care of yourself Cathy." Cherie had advised her. "And please don't ever go back to the things that can destroy you."

"I won't." Cathy had promised with a smile. "You take care of Noel and Noel, you take care of Cherie, she's one of a kind, a total sweetheart."

Just a few seconds later, once a few more smiles had been exchanged, Cathy had finally departed and that had been the last time that I had ever seen her face but over the next few months, Cherie had been sent a few postcards with updates on Cathy's transition to a clean, drug free life which she had proudly shown to me as each one had arrived.

"I guess sometimes people can change Mr. Gethin." Cherie had said one day as she had proudly showed me the third postcard. "Cathy's got a new job and she's still clean."

Not only had Cathy managed to stay clean but apparently, the woman's treatment center had also helped her to find a part time job and so I had felt some satisfaction in that at least, I'd encouraged her to change her life and that she had actually tried to do so.

"I guess they can and I guess that means, there's hope for us all Cherie." I had agreed. "Well, most of us anyway."

"Yeah, I don't think there's any hope for

people like Jonas." Cherie had swiftly agreed.

"At least she's safe now Cherie and living a better, decent life." I had concluded as I'd read the postcard a couple more times and then handed it back to her.

For once that night, I had slept one of the most peaceful nights of rest that I'd ever experienced inside the hotel, since my period of hotel ownership had actually begun because for once, there had been a pleasant outcome to an extremely negative situation. One woman had been pulled successfully from a drug infested lifestyle back into the world of normalcy and decency and that had touched my heart, my mind and my body as it had made my own problems slightly less heavy and seem far lighter to carry. Together Cherie and I had managed to convince Cathy that another life existed outside that warped, polluted world of vice and ocean of drugs and as we had given her our encouragement and support, she had grabbed onto the lifeboat of the treatment center place that had been offered to her by the hospital with every ounce of her being and then had held onto it until her life had changed.

A huge part of me had felt very encouraged by all Cathy's achievements that day because it had shown me that although negative circumstances in life can drag you down into the depths of despair, life can always lift you back up again, if you can just find and accept the lifeboats of life support on offer to you. When I reflect upon Cathy's situation, I now truly accept and realize that the lifeboats of life support on offer to us are not always easy to spot because sometimes, we can be so blinded by our own warped lifestyles, distorted perceptions, stubborn mindsets and negative behavior patterns that we miss those lifeboats entirely, don't recognize them when they appear on the horizon of our life, or even ignore them completely when they do show up. In fact, one thing I've truly learnt from that tricky, dangerous, hard situation is that life can only really offer us a lifeboat of life support, when we are actually ready to board it and when we're totally willing to accept it because at times, we can be our own barrier to a better life.

RED TAPE AND MORE RATS

Despite all my good intentions to manage and run the hotel effectively, in the end the bureaucratic red tape that I had attempted to cope with year after year had finally begun to financially cripple me because the legal stipulations and agreements that I'd entered into, coupled with my own lack of experience and knowledge had been a very rocky, turbulent partnership. In some ways it had almost felt as if a noose had been hung around my neck that had just waited patiently for the final crunch to tighten because lawyers had seemed to wait in every courtroom in the city center to financially lynch me. Financially, the situation had become increasingly difficult because the agreements and sums that I had accepted from the local authority just hadn't been enough and the income from the other guests that had stayed at the hotel had barely even scratched the surface of the general overheads, never mind covered the rest of hotel's costs and so I'd continued to operate at a loss and that loss had only grown bigger and bigger with each month that had gone by.

Unfortunately, with regards to the hotel's clientele, the problems with drugs, drunken outbursts, thievery and even prostitution had continued throughout the remainder of the second year and although I had managed to get rid of the gruesome duo that hadn't seemed to change the overall negative trend and neither had it reversed or slowed down the downward spiral. Technically yes, I had no longer had a petty crime racket on my hands and inside the interior of the building but there had been far less organized and frequent manifestations of all those criminal activities being conducted by other guests and their associates all around and even upon the premises itself and so, it had been hard to enforce any kind of order at times.

When the third year of my hotel ownership had arrived, so too had a female guest that had been allocated to the hotel by the local authority called Sandra and to be perfectly honest, I had been tempted right from the very start because she had been a pretty, mature, well-spoken woman that had brought a touch of class along with her. However, since I hadn't really dabbled in any sexual or romantic affairs with any of the guests up until that point, I had slightly feared my potential romantic involvement with Sandra purely due to my position and her own but when she had shown an interest in me, I'd really been quite flattered and had wanted to see if it might be possible to build a romantic partnership from amongst the rubble and ruins of my troubles. If Sandra had been a private client, the issue for me would have been far less clouded because private clients had the liberty to come and go as they had wished to but the situation had been far more complex, purely due to her allocation to the hotel by the local authority.

Once I had decided to jump into the romantic prospect as I'd begun to entertain the notion of a possible romance and started to acquaint myself with Sandra, I had rapidly discovered that she had been divorced several times already. A string of ex-husbands had littered Sandra's heart with all kinds of complicated, heavy baggage and so, I had definitely struggled to carry the weight of that unromantic luggage as I'd attempted to embark upon a romantic voyage with her which I had hoped would ultimately lead to the potentially pleasant destination of blissful romance. Despite Sandra's seemingly well-mannered approach however, she had demanded a lot from anyone that she had been romantically involved with and I had certainly not been an exception when it came to her attitude towards the men that stepped into her life and so the weight of romantic expectations placed upon me had rapidly grown and grown into a mountain of dissatisfied discontent.

My attempts to try and satisfy Sandra's mountain of romantic demands coupled with the unromantic emotional baggage from her previous relationships had placed me under a tremendous amount pressure and so I had almost buckled in my attempts to satisfy that mountain of demands as I'd attempted to explore a romantic partnership with her. Instead of a peaceful, pleasant, enjoyable romantic voyage however, our relationship had been more like a shipwreck of total disaster constantly stranded upon the jagged rocks of Sandra's discontent and my heart had felt as if it had been regularly crushed to pieces by the very harsh, choppy, stormy waves of her total dissatisfaction which had often been unleashed upon my heart via her cold sarcasm, angry outbursts and cruel, heartless sharp words.

Not only had Sandra wanted an abundance of material satisfaction and lots of affection but she had also demanded a lot of time from me which due to the continual stream of financial and social problems at the hotel at that point in time, had really been in quite short supply. Overall, my relationship with Sandra had definitely suffered due to the circumstances that I had faced and it had really been very strained as well as quite short lived because she had demanded things from me that I just hadn't been able to provide and so in the long term, our relationship really had been romantically unsustainable for me. Despite all the obstacles however, I had at least attempted to try and please Sandra's heart for those six months which had been the approximate duration of our entire romantic relationship but my romantic efforts had fallen well short of her very tall mountain of expectations.

Due to the huge mountain of problems that I had faced at the hotel at that time which had predominantly revolved around financial complications and disputes with the local authority, coupled with the daily chaotic drama from some of the guests, I'd definitely romantically floundered but as I reflect back at times, I realize that it had probably been for the best. Since Sandra had been very high maintenance and had harbored huge romantic expectations that had far exceeded my financial means, for approximately six months of that third year I had tried my best to appease her demands and I'd even taken out a couple of loans as I had tried to maintain the kind of lifestyle that she had expected someone in my position to be able to afford.

The perception of wealth and affluence that I had attempted to sustain and live up to however, which had predominantly been formed by Sandra's misguided expectations, had been an absolute struggle for me to maintain because it just hadn't been a true reflection of my real financial reality and so, I'd struggled to meet and live up to those illusive standards. Unfortunately, the sandy house of romance which had been built from the planks of false impressions and misguided expectations between the two of us had swiftly crashed down all around me as the debts had spiraled out of control within a few months along with the stressful worries which had not only accumulated but had also begun to crunch upon my head every single night.

Eventually, much to my sheer relief, after six stressful months that had stretched my wallet and heart as far as both had been able to go, Sandra had finally left the hotel and she had quickly latched on to another romantic partner that had been far more affluent than myself. Our sandy house of romance due to Sandra's departure had immediately totally collapsed, washed away by the tides of unromantic unpleasantness until just a few sandy grains of tarnished, stained memories had been all that remained inside my heart but as I had watched her leave my life and heart, I'd accepted my romantic defeat quite graciously.

Although a small part of me at that time had felt quite sad to see Sandra jump on to another boat of love with another pair of male hands at the helm because it had been nice to feel needed, wanted and loved for a while amongst all the harshness of daily life, I had in the end, surrendered to my romantic defeat without too many objections and without any desperate pleas for a continuation. The high expectations and unrealistic demands that had emanated from Sandra's person during that six months had not been compatible at all with my pocket or my heart, or something that I would ever have been able to satisfy and so, I had accepted my romantic losses and nursed my heart as I'd watched her not just walk away but also jump into the arms of another male suitor virtually straight away.

Since the rat, cockroach and mice infestations had continued to haunt the hotel's interior throughout that third year, I'd had to call in pest control companies several times and the latter part of the third year had been no different in that respect but when I had consulted a few local business owners about the issue, I'd discovered that such infestations had actually been a common problem for businesses in the local area. The infestation problems which had predominantly revolved around rats, mice and cockroaches had definitely been a regular source of headache and pesky occurrence at the hotel and no sooner had one bunch of pests and vermin been cleaned out than another one would suddenly appear which had been extremely costly and almost impossible for me to manage and so, those problematic issues had really frustrated me at times.

On one occasion, I can still remember being in a female guest's room where I'd had to stand on guard until an actual exterminator had arrived and that whilst I had waited, I'd had to board the rat that she had seen inside a hole in the actual skirting board in order to ensure that the vermin had no means of escape. Although to be perfectly honest what I would have done if a rat had escaped is beyond me because I had no idea how to handle such creatures and my actions probably would have just made the situation even worse.

Due to the quite long wait however, I had heard the wooden board that I'd wedged against the skirting board and placed over the hole being chewed and gnawed upon as we had waited in a united fearful silence and as I had held my breath, I'd hoped and wished that the exterminator would arrive before the rat had managed to gnaw through the wood. From my point of view, although mice hadn't really been regarded as a huge, major issue for me, rats had been a totally different kettle of fish, simply because rats as I had already known, could be far more vicious and rats could and would actually bite people.

The female guest who had been in her mid-sixties and called Maggie had been a polite, well-mannered woman that had been as quiet as a mouse and since she had seemed to scare very easily as the seconds had ticked away, I had kept my eyes diligently glued to the boarded-up hole in the corner of the room and had remained on active guard. Nothing but the gnaws of the rat and our heavy breath which had been laden with tension had been heard inside the room as we had waited as the rat's teeth had continued to grate against the wooden board but neither of us it had seemed, had dared to make a single sound which on my part had mainly been because I had not wanted to miss any developments in the rat's movements.

When the exterminator had finally arrived, I had rushed downstairs with Maggie in tow since she'd had absolutely no desire to stay inside her guest room with just the rat inside the hole for company and the gnaws which had still continued even as we had stepped out of the room because as she'd openly admitted to me as we'd walked, the noises from the rat had really scared her. Since that particular extermination company had been called to the premises several times prior to that day, I had been on first name terms with the manager of the company and so the man that had been sent to the hotel on that particular occasion, who I'd also met before on at least one occasion, had given me a wide, friendly smile as I had shown him into the premises and had then escorted him to the Maggie's guest room which had been situated on the second floor. Once the exterminator, who had been called Marcus, had been shown into Maggie's guest room, I had then led him towards the corner of the room where the rat had been trapped behind the wooden board and Marcus had quickly set to work as he had immediately started to put on some leather gloves.

"How many rats do you think there are behind this skirting board Mr. Gethin?" Marcus had asked.

"As far as I know there should only be one." I had replied but some doubts had lain inside my mind as I'd turned to face Maggie and sought further clarity. "How many rats did you see Maggie?"

"I just saw one Mr. Gethin." Maggie had said as her voice had cracked with tension and she had glanced at the skirting board nervously. She had turned to face Marcus before she'd continued. "Do you think there could be more than one in there?"

"Well, at times you do get a whole family of rats inside a building and sometimes, more than just one family." Marcus had explained. "Usually it just depends on how much food can be sourced easily and the easier it is, the more frequently rats will gather inside a building and then actually stay."

For a few minutes as Marcus had knelt down beside the skirting board with the trap and a small hammer clasped in his hands, I had held my breath as I'd watched him but as I had glanced back up at Maggie's face, I'd quickly given her a certain nod of reassurance despite all my fears. However, as soon as the wooden board had been lifted up, a rat had darted straight out of it and the creature had somehow managed to completely avoid the trap but as it had paused, twitched its nose in the air and then had tried to dash across the room, Marcus had reacted swiftly and had grabbed the rodent by the scruff off the neck as the small hammer had been swiftly raised and then slammed down against the rat's head and body.

A loud crunch had sounded out all around us and as the vibrations had flown across the room, the rat had released a very loud shriek and as I had seen Maggie wince in a total disgust, I'd sighed with sheer relief. Nothing but a shocked silence had suddenly seemed to fill the entire room for a few seconds as I had looked at Maggie's face and the horrified expression upon it but no sooner had Marcus hit the first creature over the head than just a few seconds later, another two rats had darted out of the hole and had then shot across the room.

Due to the unexpected appearance of two more rats, a very loud shriek had immediately flown from Maggie's mouth as she had suddenly rushed towards her bed and then jumped on top of it but Marcus, I had observed, had remained totally calm as he had taken the appearance of the other two rats totally in his stride and had just reached for his equipment hold-all and for another trap box. The first trap I had noticed, Marcus had already placed close to the actual hole in the skirting board and it faced the actual skirting board itself but as I'd watched him work, he had secured it more tightly and snugly against the wall and then another trap had swiftly been laid right next to it which had faced in the opposite direction.

Once those two traps had been adjusted and securely laid, Marcus had then plucked a few more traps from his hold-all and had risen to his feet as he'd prepared to set some more traps across the floor in other parts of the room.

“Those two traps should catch any other rats that might try to come out of that hole, or any that try to return to their hiding place.” Marcus had explained as he had begun to stride across the room with the empty traps inside his hands. “So, all I have to do now is to try and lure the two rats that have already escaped towards these traps."

For approximately the next thirty minutes I had watched and waited as Marcus had chased the other two rats around the room and once he had filled his two traps and he'd finished with Maggie's guest room, Marcus had then come to a standstill directly in front of me and had turned to face me.

"Do you think that's all of them Mr. Gethin?" Marcus had asked as he had picked up his hold-all. "Has anyone seen rats anywhere else in the building, perhaps on one of the other floors?"

"I have." Maggie had swiftly replied. "I saw one in the bathroom on the ground floor just the other day."

"Right. Well if you'd like me to Mr. Gethin, I can set some more traps there for you now?" Marcus had immediately offered. "Usually rats and mice are very territorial, they tend to stick to certain areas in a building, so it's quite possible that the other rat sighting involved another rat or even another group of rats."

"Yes thanks, that's a good idea Marcus. What can I do in the long term to keep them out of the building?" I had asked.

“Well Mr. Gethin, first and foremost you should advise all your guests not to keep or consume any food inside their rooms because the scraps attract all kinds of pests and vermin.” Marcus had explained as he had pointed towards some empty cake wrappers filled with cake crumbs. “The crumbs and scraps attract rats, mice and other pests and then they settle around the food source but I have to say, your battle with the rats and other pests is far from over because this area is well known for not only rats but also mice and cockroaches. You can also try to block any holes that you can find but sometimes, rats will gnaw through pieces of wood and mice can squeeze through the tiniest of spaces, so it can be very difficult." He had mentioned as he'd started to walk towards the door of the guest room.

"Thanks so much." Maggie had said appreciatively.

"No problem, if you can just show me where you saw the other rat in the bathroom please then I can deal with them all in one visit." Marcus had replied.

“Sure.” Maggie had agreed.

Just as a few seconds later we had all left Maggie's room and then had begun to walk towards the ground floor bathroom and as I had walked, I'd scanned the stairs, halls and landings for any possible holes or rats. On our way towards the ground floor Marcus had discussed rats as we had walked and their usual lifestyles and some of his observations and comments had absolutely horrified and totally repulsed me, purely due to the very unhygienic implications.

“You know Mr. Gethin, rats are really quite sociable creatures and so it’s highly unlikely that this family of rats would be living here alone inside your guest house." Marcus had explained. "There’s probably a whole community of them hiding under the floorboards of this building and under some of the other buildings in this street.”

"Now that is not a pleasant thought." I had replied.

The thought of a whole community of vermin scattered across different parts of the hotel under the floorboards, across the entire street and even sprinkled across the back garden had made me feel quite nauseous because that possibility had meant only one thing for me, more expensive pest control extermination visits. Another worry that had also concerned me at the time had been the fact that rats had been known to bite people which had meant that if one of the guests had crossed a rat's path and then they tried to tackle the creature alone, they might even end up getting badly bitten and injured and that potential negative eventuality had really worried me.

Much to my absolute horror, the bathroom on the ground floor had turned out to be just as infested as Maggie's room because no sooner had we stepped inside the room than I had seen a rat scurry across the floor directly in front of our faces just before the creature had hidden inside a hole in the skirting boards. Since some loud squeaks had emanated from the floorboards below my feet, I had almost winced in disgust as Marcus had swiftly begun to inspect the area and then had nodded his head.

"I think there's a whole family of rats in this room under the floorboards Mr. Gethin." Marcus had swiftly concluded. "If I can lift up one of the floorboards I might be able to get them all in one go and that'll save me from having to come back later this week."

"Yep, do whatever you need to do Marcus." I had rapidly agreed.

In a matter of just minutes Marcus had walked over to the other side of the bathroom and then he had quickly pulled up the relevant floorboard with one of his tools and rather shockingly, I had horrifyingly discovered that there had actually been three rats nestled in-between the wooden beams under the floorboard. The three rats' bodies had been coiled snugly around each other into that quite small space in the depths of the floor in-between two wooden beams and as we had watched them for a few seconds in shocked surprise, I had listened to the creatures as the rats had seemed to squabble amongst themselves. Since the creatures' garbled arguments had only consisted of purely ratish shrieks, none of which our human ears could have ever hoped to understand even if we had wanted to, I had shaken my head in total disgust as we'd all just stood and had listened to the rats for a few seconds in shocked silence.

"I can't watch this Mr. Gethin." Maggie had said as she had suddenly shuddered and then had shaken her head. "Yuck, it's too much for me. I really hate rats and mice, I think I'll leave you guys to it." She had insisted just before she'd swiftly fled from the room.

Irrespective of Maggie's sudden desertion, Marcus and I had remained inside the bathroom as I'd watched him deal with the three rats for approximately the next thirty minutes and once the three rats had been removed from between the wooden beams and placed inside traps, another couple of traps had been laid inside the communal bathroom. Before Marcus had finally departed, I had also shown him into the communal kitchen and adjoined lounge area where he had laid some more traps in that adjoined space as well some in other nooks and crannies around the building inclusive of the main cleaning cupboard, the landings and some had even been laid upon the stairs.

Finally, after more than a good hour and a half had gone by since Marcus's initial arrival, he had left the building and as I had seen him off and to the front door, I'd sighed a very heavy, weary, defeated sigh. A hotel that had housed rats, mice and cockroaches in every possible nook and cranny hadn't been my idea of a decent provision when it came to actual accommodation and so the reality of what Marcus had discovered that day throughout his visit had weighed heavily upon my mind.

Although I hadn't aimed for the Happyvale Hotel to be a top five-star establishment because quite frankly, I really hadn't possessed the means or financial resources to achieve that goal, I had at least hoped to provide a decent, safe place for guests to rest their head in a vermin and pest free environment and so in that respect, I'd definitely, totally and utterly failed. So many guests had flowed through the hotel's front door and had resided inside the hotel's walls over the years but shockingly that day I had discovered, so too had some uninvited rats and those creatures I'd begun to realize, had probably visited and spent just as much time upon the premises as the guests themselves as the rats had occupied the spaces underneath the floorboards probably as frequently as the human guests that had come and gone.

Despite my partial victory with the rats that day however, unfortunately for me over those three years, the fluidity in movement when it had come to the local authority guests had not been applicable to the actual movements of Mike Walker and very frustratingly, he had remained my main point of contact in the employment ranks of the local authority over the next decade and beyond. Numerous tricky, complex, bureaucratic disputes had taken place over those next ten years between us both because Mike had seemed to be totally oblivious to the often-outlandish conduct and drug related problems that had been so prevalent amongst many of the clients that he had sent to my hotel to be temporarily housed. At times I had even wondered if Mike Walker had known the reality but just hadn't cared because most of the time, it had seemed as if all he had cared about had been the targets that he'd been set that he had to meet for the performance of his own job and it often felt as if he'd dumped every antisocial, difficult client upon my shoulders that he had been presented with.

In terms of my personal sentiments towards Mike Walker, I had loathed him right from the very start but that dislike hadn't been singular and had always been mutual though how it had actually begun, I can barely recall but from what I remember, he had just always been a very harsh, stern, unlikable man and so we had always clashed. Our contempt for each other had not reduced over the years, neither had our regular verbal clashes and disputes over guests, damages to hotel property and repair bills and his complaints about the condition of the hotel had been a constant thorn in my side as the years had gone by which had definitely been exasperated and aggravated even more by the difficult clients that he had sent through the hotel's front door. Unfortunately, all I had ever experienced from Mike Walker since our first encounter had been a stiff, rigid, regimented approach and it had almost been as if the money to pay for the guest rooms that the local authority had provided had come out of his own pocket because he really had been so very tough, tight and stingy and he hadn't really seemed to give two hoots about the actual clients themselves.

One of the worst encounters and disputes that I'd had with Mike Walker as I reflect back over our turbulent interactions had actually involved a guest that had come to the hotel in my thirteenth year of my hotel ownership and due to the conduct of the guest, I had almost hit the roof. From what I had heard from some of the female guests, shortly after this particular male guest had arrived he had been seen out and about in the local area on the prowl and the man who had been in his late fifties had approached several young women who he'd attempted to ply with alcohol and drugs in order to sexually exploit them. Since I had discovered that several of the young women in question had been brought back to the hotel and had even been ushered into his guest room in a drugged up, drunken state, I'd raised the issue with him, confronted him directly and had even verbally objected to his conduct but he had simply denied the allegations made by the female guests and had even continued.

After several specific incidents had been reported to me by other guests, I had reluctantly contacted Mike Walker to demand that the man who had been called Humphrey should be moved from the hotel immediately, since he had clearly been a sexual predator but all I'd been met with had been a wall of absolute and total refusal. Just as I had expected when I'd spoken to Mike Walker, he had been totally uncooperative and due to the very serious nature of my complaints, his attitude had frustrated the absolute hell out of me.

"Without proof Mr. Gethin, I can't move him." Mike Walker had insisted in a stern tone.

"But he's a sexual predator." I had complained.

"Until you can prove it, he won't be moved." Mike Walker had snapped.

"What about the female guests?" I had asked.

"Look, it's your hotel, how you manage difficult customers is entirely up to you." Mike Walker had replied sarcastically.

"He's more than just a difficult guest, he is plying young women with drugs and alcohol and then he's bringing them back to this hotel to sexually exploit them." I had urged.

"The only thing I can suggest is that you

ban him from bringing any guests into the hotel." Mike Walker had said.

"That would mean that I would have to watch him night and day to enforce that rule." I had replied.

"That's really not my problem Mr. Gethin and the only time that will change is if you have proof." Mike Walker had insisted in an adamant tone.

"There are a few female guests that have seen him bring some of the young women to the hotel." I had quickly pointed out.

"That wouldn't be enough, you would have to prove that sexual contact had occurred and that drugs and alcohol had actually been utilized as a form of coercion." Mike Walker had insisted sarcastically. "These are very serious allegations and so you would have to prove every single one before I could take any further action. Now, if that's all Mr. Gethin, I really have to get on with my working day."

"Right." I had replied in a defeated tone but as I'd ended the call, I had seethed inside.

Much to my absolute horror, it had actually taken me three whole months in the end to convince Mike Walker to finally move Humphrey along and it had only really happened at all because I had managed to involve another housing officer that had pressured him to do so. The red tape when it came to local authority clients had been problematic but Mike Walker coupled with the bureaucracy had been a nightmarish hell that had made my hotel almost totally unbearable to live in not only for the guests but also for myself.

In terms of financially over that ten years, things had become increasingly difficult for me and so I had borrowed money time and time again just to make ends meet and to make urgent building repairs and so, my debt levels had grown and grown and had almost spiraled through the hotel's roof. Although I had always utilized various forms of credit in order to finance the hotel's operations and to plug the short-term gaps ever since I had taken actual ownership of the hotel, the gaps had grown significantly wider and far bigger over that decade and as I'd reached my fifteenth year of my hotel ownership, I had arrived at that point in time with a massive accumulation of debt.

A lack of respect for the premises on the part of the guests that the hotel had housed and the reduced local authority rates which had not taken into consideration any long-term maintenance costs and building repairs had been factors that had definitely taken their toll upon the Happyvale Hotel's four walls and so, I had really struggled at times to keep the hotel financially afloat. At one point towards the end of that first fifteen years, I had even had to borrow a huge lump sum which had been secured against the property itself, just to pay for some necessary building repairs but it hadn't even touched the tip of any potential improvements and so improvements to the hotel's interior or exterior had remained totally out of my financial reach and completely out of the question. The road of good intentions as I had sadly discovered by the fifteenth year of my hotel ownership, could definitely lead to total disaster and although I had wanted the Happyvale Hotel to be a decent place to live, a successful hotel, a positive environment and profitable, unfortunately the weight of the financial responsibilities had grown and grown until I had ended up in huge amounts of debt. Very frustratingly, the capital sums from the loans that I had already taken had not even touched the surface of the hotel's problems and had only just been enough to sustain the sub-standard provisions on offer but those financial burdens had remained and had remained very tightly tied to my side as I'd continued to struggle with the hotel's operational and financial losses.

THE BATTLE

After the fifteenth year had gone by which in some respects had been a significant milestone for me, my quasi-corporate dealings, semi-professional relationship and guest related interactions with the local authority had continued to slide even further down the slippery slope of stressful antagonism. The main reason for that downward trend I had mainly attributed to the fact that Mike Walker had remained in a position of power and so he had remained responsible for all of the local authority's dealings with my hotel and since our personalities had definitely conflicted and clashed which had resulted in nothing but total stress, I had of course borne the brunt of that stress on my slight shoulders. Unfortunately, over the next five years that relationship had deteriorated even further because Mike Walker had remained in his post and had even been promoted which I had hoped at one point might result in a change in my situation but very frustratingly and rather annoyingly, he had still continued to be my main point of contact.

The relationship between Mike Walker and I had almost been like a rotten tooth that had sat inside a mouth with decayed roots for a prolonged period of time with absolutely no dental treatment and nothing it had seemed had been able to change those rotten roots which had been formed from our mutual, total contempt for each other. Absolutely nothing had been able to restore that rotten tooth and the only possibility that could have perhaps changed that state of rotten, contemptuous decay would perhaps have been if either Mike Walker or myself had wished to be the extraction but since neither of us had it seemed, any intentions of being removed, we had both still remained in our respective positions for two decades and so he had remained a thorn in my side and an ugly crack in the hotel's walls for that entire period of time.

Due to Mike Walker and his problematic attitude, my battle with the local authority had definitely deepened as the first twenty years of my hotel ownership had come to an end, by which point I had begun to realize that my options to try and salvage the hotel had shrunk as my debts and the costs of regulatory compliance had grown. The regulations that had been implemented by the local authority as the years had gone by had increased significantly and as a result, my wallet had not only been stretched but also almost strangled by the bureaucracy and the costs that had to be incurred to adhere to those stricter, much tighter conditions which by the end of the twentieth year had almost, totally crippled me financially. Despite the avalanche of difficulties that had lurked just above my head each morning that had threatened to fall on top of me and bury me under the rocks of financial destitution every day however, I had tried to stand up for the hotel that my mother had given so much of her life to and had persevered as I'd attempted to face the courtrooms and to challenge the legalities that had knocked upon my door along with the strangleholds of bureaucracy that had gripped the hotel and my life, purely due to my acceptance of local authority clients.

When it had come to the actual issues upon the premises itself and the clientele that had occupied the hotel's walls, things had pretty much continued in the same manner despite the many legal battles, all the stressful turbulence and financial turmoil in that the vermin had continued to plague the premises and the guests had continued to treat the hotel pretty much as they had wished to. Another huge loan had been secured against the premises to conduct essential repair works to the building in that twentieth year and to fight some of the legal battles, the costs of which had rapidly escalated and snowballed significantly and so, I had hardly been able to rest my head at night due to the worries about how that large debt would be satisfied. The financial reality had been that the hotel had not made enough money to cover adherence to the local authority's regulations and stipulations which had grown over the years and so I had struggled to meet the general overheads as I'd waded my way through the stormy, choppy waves of financial turmoil for the entire five years.

In terms of the actual guests that had occupied the hotel in those days, the customer base had definitely become much harder over the years and far wilder and so, I had often found it difficult to keep and maintain any kind of order inside the hotel itself. The days of pleasant guests like Cherie, Noel and Tom had definitely long gone by that point and the majority of the guests that Mike Walker had sent to the hotel had predominantly been more like the ratbags Mario, Pervy Pete, Vernon, Jonas and Humphrey and that continual allocation of mainly very difficult, antisocial customers had continued to not only frustrate me but had also really stressed me out.

Although I had started to fight the costly regulatory stipulations that had been enforced upon me and the fines that had been inflicted due to my failure to comply with those regulations in full and I'd even consulted several lawyers in that twentieth year, I had almost crumbled due to the tremendous pressure that had been placed upon my mind. In many ways, it had felt as if I had been jammed in-between a solid rock of pure hate in the form of Mike Walker and a boulder of trouble in the form of the costly regulatory adherence that I had been unable to meet purely due to the lower guest room rates that had hardly increased over the years and so, I'd been trapped in an absolutely impossible situation which I had been unable to retrieve either myself or the hotel from with any dignity.

The stressful tight knots of costly regulatory compliance from the local authority as I had known at the time, would not be loosened and if anything would only become far worse and much tighter in the future because I'd been unable to make the necessary and required improvements to the building due to financial constraints and so total frustration had set in. Every second of my life had seemed to be caught in a circular loop of negativity and the problems that had continued to drag the hotel downwards which had borne no actual signs of any possible recovery.

Twenty years of my hotel ownership had evaporated and the only remnants and residue that had been left behind had been a huge pile of debts and a hotel that had been on the brink of total financial collapse. Every direction that I had faced in those days had been laden with trouble, stress, drama and headache and I'd virtually had no means of escape because no escape hatch had existed and there had been no peaceful place of sanctuary to provide some relief from the problems that had hung over my head since the hotel had been my actual home. The daily outbursts of erratic and outlandish behavior upon the premises itself had continued and if anything had become far worse because most of the guests that the local authority had sent to me at that time had often lacked any kind of physical restraint and so, I had struggled to control, manage and contend with my daily load which had unfortunately, also included the frequent, angry physical confrontations between guests that had usually been rooted in drug related disputes and alcohol induced arguments.

Somehow, it had almost felt as if I had fallen or had been pushed into a deep abyss of problems and as if the vultures had started to swoop down into the abyss to pick at my flesh every single day and I'd been unable to escape that abyss because no ladder of support or rope of friendship had been thrown towards me and so, I had sunk further and further down into the quicksand of hardship that the ground below my feet seemed to have been formed from. In terms of support there had been virtually none since everywhere I had turned or faced at that time had been vested with self-interest and as I reflect back, I remember that some people had even longed to see my failure and downfall which had meant that I'd really struggled to trust anyone.

Anyone and everyone that had crossed my path at that time or that had come in close proximity to me, it had seemed had sensed the financial shipwreck that I had been aboard and had then sought to pick off any fleshy wealth that they could from the bones of my failure and so, I'd definitely struggled to find any real allies in life. Since I hadn't really lived my life in a very considerate manner up until that point and I'd spent a lot of time around people that hadn't given a dam about anyone else, I had never really learnt how to accommodate and support other people's needs, how to build trustworthy relationships or how to create effective support systems of friendship and for the first time in my life that failure to establish constructive human relationships had really mattered. Although I had searched and hoped and wished and waited, no rescue boat had however, ever come my way or had appeared upon the horizon of my life and not only had my boat of life fully capsized but it had also remained shipwrecked upon the rocks of destruction in a torn, crushed, delipidated state as stormy wave after stormy wave of problems had lashed against it from all directions possible because unfortunately, no trusted lighthouse keeper had ever shone a light out in that darkness to save my boat or me.

Despite all the difficulties however, I had continued to try to hold onto the hotel as the next three years had gone by as I'd accepted that I had made a lot of mistakes and that I'd really lacked the knowledge, experience and skills to make the Happyvale Hotel into a decent place to stay that had managed to generate an actual profit. The numerous legal battles had continued throughout those three years and although I had tried to take a final stand as I'd fought each and every single one and I had even somehow managed to juggle the huge mountains of debt, the bailiffs had constantly remained just a step away from my door throughout that entire three years. Although I had been way out of my depth and by that point had almost sunk to the very bottom of the ocean of problems that I'd set sail upon when I had assumed ownership of the hotel, I'd still hoped that something would eventually turn in my favor and that all the damage that had been done over those twenty-three years, would somehow be reversed.

When I had initially assumed ownership of the hotel, I hadn't been provided with any guidelines or an instruction manual and sadly, my mother hadn't been around to advise me, support me, assist me or even to warn me about anything that might happen, if I had decided to follow a particular course of action and so I'd made many, many mistakes. Since I had failed to build any other support networks in life that might have provided a safety net of support or even just a bit of sincere guidance and impartial advice to me, I'd really struggled to find a port of friendship during those very difficult years and so I had simply existed on the brink of total failure engulfed in legal battles as I'd continued to sink. At times I had felt as if there had been no one at all that I'd been able to place an ounce of trust in because it had seemed like everyone around me had just wanted to cash in and scavenge for any potential wealth that they may have been able to lay their hands on from the hotel's collapse and my failure which had lurked upon the very near horizon of my life every single day.

Sincerity on the part of those around me since I had assumed ownership of the hotel had seemed to be in such short supply but I had blamed myself in part for that shortfall because I'd never really valued sincerity before, or ever really understood its true value and possibly at times, I hadn't even had the ability to recognize true sincerity when it had shown up. In fact, prior to my ownership of the hotel, I had pretty much stumbled through life and I'd never really possessed something of my own before that had been so valuable and since I had been totally under-equipped to cope with that responsibility, some words of wisdom, friendly arms of support and some sincere guidance that had truly had my best interests at heart had been desperately needed but it had been so hard for me to find those things, to recognize such invaluable human provisions and to place my trust in anyone around me.

For the most part throughout those difficult three years, I had struggled to rest at night due to not only the incessant financial worries, the conditions of the tight regulatory compliance but also because of the arguments that had kicked off inside the hotel's four walls on a daily basis most of which had revolved around drug and alcohol related misunderstandings between guests. Since the hotel had been my only home and the only home that I'd ever really known however, I had been unable to leave the premises and so I'd had to live each day fully immersed in my predicament and I had just had to cope with the drunken, drugged up, rowdy outbursts from some of the guests. Most of the guests that had possessed even a scrap of decency that had stepped through the hotel's front door during those three years had fled from the hotel's interior as soon as they had been able to and some had even pressured the local authority to move them more quickly as they had cited the violent drug and alcohol related outbursts as a danger to their safety and the pest infestations as a health hazard.

Deep down inside at that point in time, I had already known that I'd been involved in a battle that I had been highly unlikely to win but I'd been unable to surrender or to retreat because I hadn't wanted to lose the hotel that had been in my family's possession for generations and there really had been nowhere else to go and nothing else to retreat to or to hide behind. The final responsibility for the failure or success of the Happyvale Hotel had lain at my doorstep every morning and at the foot of my bed each night and even now, I still remember some of the tedious legal battles that I had gone through as I'd tried to keep hope alive, the hotel in my family's possession and a roof over my head.

Everything inside the hotel had looked tarnished, dull, old, worn, dismal, damaged and torn but there had been no money to replace anything or to freshen up the hotel's interior because every spare penny had to be spent upon debts and legal fees as I had attempted to keep the hotel in my hands. Several guests in those three years had asked me when the worn out and torn items or the broken furniture would be replaced but I had been unable to provide any answers to them and had spent most of my time inside the building shut inside my room as I'd attempted to avoid contact with people as much as I had been able to.

My life and the hotel had been on the brink of absolute financial meltdown and total collapse for those entire three years and the legal demands that had hovered over my head which had swooped through my letterbox every single day had continued very consistently and relentlessly. The only real choice I'd had at that time, since I had been unable to find any other solutions that would allow me to repair and restore the hotel's run down state, had been to face the legal challenges and to fight each one, even though that course of action had cost me even more money in the end and money that I really hadn't had and definitely hadn't been able to afford. Despite all the hardships I had faced however, I'd continued to fight but as I had done so, I'd continued to incur huge legal costs which had changed absolutely nothing because the building itself had been in such a rundown state and that damaged, delipidated condition had gone against me in every way that it possibly could have.

In my twenty third year of hotel ownership as usual, an inspector from the local authority or a third-party contractor that they had outsourced the task to had visited the hotel to test the fire alarms, safety equipment and fire exits which had happened pretty consistently up until that point in time and so in that respect, the twenty third year had been no exception. On the day of the first scheduled appointment, a woman called June Wellbury who I had met a few times before had attended the premises one Monday morning in the latter part of the year. Since June had not filled in the paperwork in a manner that had satisfied Mike Walker's standards however, he had then sent her back to the hotel three times that week to dot and cross every single letter on the inspection sheet and so she had wearily complied and to be perfectly honest, I had actually felt quite sorry for her by the third visit. On June's third and final visit which had happened on the Friday afternoon of that same week, she had finally voiced her opinions to me about Mike Walker and had complained to me about the stress from his end as I had shown her around the building once again which I'd definitely been able to relate to.

"It's a lot of work Mr. Gethin, I've never had a boss like him before. He is very precise and extremely rigid." June Wellbury had moaned. "And my workload is absolutely huge because I have so many inspections to perform in one week, so I really can't be traipsing back and forth to redo the same one three times."

"Yes, Mike Walker and I certainly aren't the best of friends." I had acknowledged.

"When Mike Walker was promoted, he was put in charge of all the safety inspections and ever since then my working hours have been a total nightmare and my workload has grown and grown into a mountain of demands." June had complained. "He's just demands so much from everyone and it's not even realistic."

"I know, I notice that every time he sends a new client to the hotel." I had agreed.

For once I had felt slightly relieved by an inspection officer's attendance which had been highly unusual because usually I'd dreaded their appearances but June Wellbury had provided me with some comfort that day and that week because she too it had transpired had been a victim of Mike Walker's harshness and his difficult demands. However, as I had also been very much aware at the time, June Wellbury's complaints about Mike Walker hadn't been enough to change my situation or the financial predicament that I'd faced because the losses from the hotel had grown and grown each year and the snowball effect had gathered as debts upon debts had accumulated along the way which had added to the general financial shortfalls from the hotel's operations.

The practicalities of my agreements with the local authority had just not added up and the hotel's revenue from the local authority clients had not covered all the costs of those basic accommodation provisions and although there had been other guests, the additional income had not been enough to make up for those consistent negative financial shortfalls.

In some respects however, I had felt as I'd almost made an ally that day because June Wellbury and I had found some common ground and that common ground which had united us both to some extent had been the hard solid cement of Mike Walker's sharp manner, the rockiness of his harsh rigid approach and the stony cruelness of his sarcastic tongue which had at times, been razor sharp and almost like a verbal whip that had cut into your ears and mind.

Towards the end of that twenty third year as I had waded through courtrooms, lawyers and numerous bailiff's visits, the hotel had transcended into even more of a pigsty as I'd heard a shriek one morning from the ground floor bathroom and had rushed to the communal area to inspect the source of alarm. Unlike the previous cockroach infestations this one however, had been more like an insect invasion and at least ten cockroaches had been spotted around the room as a lady called Patty in her mid-forties had performed her daily hygiene routine early that morning. Unfortunately, since my financial position had been really quite strained at that time, on that particular occasion I had decided to try and deal with the pests myself which in hindsight hadn't really been a wise decision at all on my part.

Later that morning I had begun to prepare myself for my mission as I'd popped out to the local hardware store and bought some Polyfilla, overalls and some cockroach traps and spray which apparently, I had to lay and spray all over the bathroom floor and walls and so as soon as I'd returned to the hotel, I had enthusiastically put on the overalls that I'd just purchased. On my way towards the bathroom I had bumped into a male guest called Sam who had been a local authority client in his mid-thirties and he had laughed at my outfit and he had also mentioned the cockroaches in the bathroom which he too had noticed.

"You know Mr. Gethin, I saw at least five cockroaches in the bathroom today when I took my bath this morning, this really must be the worst hotel in Britain and its probably the worst hotel that I've ever stayed in." Sam had acknowledged as a feisty grin had crossed his face. "How are you going to get rid of them?"

"Don't worry Sam, I've got the situation under control." I had replied confidently even though deep down inside, I'd been situated a million miles away from my confident tone.

"Okay but if you need any help just let me know. I have a friend that can knock those cockroaches out in a jiffy but it will cost you though." Sam had replied in a cocky tone.

"Right thanks Sam, I'll let you know." I had replied as I'd opened up the bathroom door and then stepped inside the room.

Although I hadn't really wanted to deal with the pests myself, I had really been in a very tight financial fix and so I'd quickly set to work with the packet of Polyfilla and some cockroach traps and bait which I had quickly spread out and laid around the room. For the remainder of that morning I had tended solely to the cockroach problem as I'd sealed off the bathroom and put a sign on the door so that no guests would attempt to utilize it for any purpose and as far as I had been concerned, I'd dealt with the issue effectively, swiftly and appropriately. However later that day, I had felt some strange pains in my stomach which had almost crippled me and in the middle of the afternoon, Ursula who had remained with me despite all the years that had gone by, the financial dramas and the fluctuations in guests had noticed my condition and so, she had advised me to rest.

"You should really try to rest Mr. Gethin and if it continues, maybe you should see a doctor." Ursula had advised.

Since I had really felt quite poorly at that point in time, I'd agreed with her advice and so I had followed it straight away and had spent the rest of that day inside my room but by the time the next morning had arrived, I'd felt even worse and so I had decided to call a doctor.

"Look Mr. Gethin, if you can't make it to Doctor Patterson's surgery this morning or this afternoon then you'll have to call back later today to request the out of hours service. Once you've done that we can send someone round but you might have to wait for hours." The doctor's receptionist had advised me on the phone.

"That's okay, I can wait. Right now, I can't

even walk around." I had agreed.

At around lunchtime that day Ursula had brought me some chicken soup and some fresh bread and as she had sympathized with my pain, she had even sat with me for thirty minutes whilst I had consumed it. Despite all my legal and financial woes, Ursula had stood with me and had stayed in employment at the hotel, even when things had been very tricky financially and she had at times, even waited up to two or three months to be paid and for her steadfast loyalty, I had felt extremely appreciative. In so many ways, Ursula had been a pillar of strength over the years to not just myself but also to the hotel because she had held the roof of the hotel over my head as she'd maintained a sense of normality throughout all the chaotic turbulence which at times, had motivated and encouraged me to continue but she had never actually been someone that I had confided in about the problems that I had faced, purely due to our positions and my position as her employer. From my point of view, I hadn't wanted to worry Ursula about the things that she had not been responsible for and so, I hadn't involved her in any of the legal complexities or confided in her over the years as I had kept the hotel's problems pretty much to myself and had just attempted to cope.

Once the early evening had arrived, just like the receptionist had advised me to earlier that day, I had called the doctor's surgery again and had requested the out of hours service and the woman on the phone had agreed to send one of the emergency-out-of-hours doctors to the hotel. Approximately four hours later and at almost ten that night, the doctor had finally shown up and had arrived on the hotel's front doorstep and as I had walked to the door and then shown him in, I'd almost doubled over in pain with every step because my stomach had been in absolute turmoil.

For the next ten minutes and as the doctor had physically examined me, I had lain down completely still upon my bed and then he had begun to ask me a series of questions which had mainly revolved around the foods that I'd eaten or the things that I had done over the past couple of days and just prior to the pains in my stomach. Since I had tended to the cockroaches, just before the stomach pains had started, I'd then shown him the packages of the Polyfilla, poison bait and traps that I had utilized and he had immediately shaken his head as he'd inspected the packaging of each item.

"I think you might have ended up poisoning yourself Mr. Gethin." The doctor had advised. "Look, I'll give you something now which might neutralize the affects slightly and a prescription to pick up tomorrow morning from the local chemist. You have to be very careful though when you handle such dangerous substances and in future, you should really wear some protective gloves."

From that day forth I had never ever attempted to perform any type of pest control activities upon the premises again myself because I'd truly learnt the lesson that sometimes, when you try to cut a corner financially, you can end up in a worse state than the one you started in. Although everything around me had been in a state of total legal turmoil and absolute financial chaos at that time, I had from that experience started to appreciate that at least I'd still had my health and I had found some comfort in the fact that I'd still been able to live an active life because that experience in life had truly taught me the value of both those things which before that point, I had so often taken for granted.

Unlike the doctor's visit which had provided me with much needed medical assistance however, the legal difficulties had continued and the hotel had continued to deteriorate in every way that it had been possible to do so. The lawyers had only been able to prolong and delay the problems but they had not been able to find an actual legal solution to any of the problematic issues that I had faced as the next year had gone by and I had continued to fight for the hotel and to keep the hotel under my ownership.

My life had become a total wreckage, the hotel a shattered dream of wealth and my hotel ownership an act of homage to my mother that had no chance on the face of the planet of actual, successful realization. Everywhere I had turned people had seemed to mock my downfall and failure and my biggest foe, Mike

Walker had truly prevailed because I'd been on my knees in the gutter as I had buckled time and time again under the sheer weight of the troubles that had littered every minute and that had plagued second of my life. The days of luxury and steak dinners with bottles of wine had fled a long time ago and all that had replaced those once happier days had been bailiff threats, inspection orders and legal summons. Sleep had no longer been a peaceful place for me each night and instead nightmares rooted in worries had flooded through my mind whenever I had tried to rest and my mind had tossed and turned every single night in sleepless discomfort due to the stress.

FINAL EXIT

For the next year or so the legal battles had virtually paralyzed me because I had forked out time and time again for lawyers but it hadn't made a scrap of difference and as the twenty fifth year had been ushered in, I'd had to face the reality that the hotel I had fought so hard to save and keep would probably no longer be my home or even belong to me by the end of that year. Despite the probability that I would lose the hotel however, I had tried to fight for the hotel as the first quarter of the year had slipped by.

In every sense of the word, I had totally floundered and I'd not even managed to build a decent relationship to keep me on an even keel through the rough times or over the bumpy, rocky hardships and there had been no remnants of comfort to be found in life because the hotel had been my whole life for so very long. When it had come to romantic relationships, most of the women that had shown me any interest over those years had either been in pursuit of wealth that they had mistakenly thought I had possessed which I definitely hadn't or they'd lost interest in me quite quickly because the hotel had demanded so much of my time since it had been such a huge part of my life and such a huge part of me.

From day to day, things had pretty much continued in the same way throughout the first part of that year but towards the middle of the year there had been far less guests in occupancy at the hotel, due to the financial pressures from the more deeply frayed and strained relationships with the local authority and less private clients had stayed because the hotel had looked more rundown than ever. Financially, things had continued to deteriorate as the year had gone on and my focus had become the constant legal battles and financial debts instead of guest occupancy and the provision of actual accommodation.

Just a handful of guests had remained at the hotel and those clients had mainly been local authority clients because to be perfectly honest, not many private clients had been willing to pay the going rate for a room in those days because the state of the rooms and interior of the building had deteriorated so much by that point. Despite the fact that only a handful of guests had remained upon the premises however, and that finances had been very tight, I had tried my best to soldier on as usual and keep things on an even keel, even though things had been far from normal and the hotel had been on the brink of financial collapse and actual total shutdown.

When it had come to the actual issue of the guests themselves, a very unusual incident had occurred in that final year which had involved a guest called Alfie who had been a quiet man in his late fifties that had stayed at the hotel for about six months. Unlike many of the other local authority clients that had walked through the front door throughout that last five years however, Alfie had always been regarded as less troublesome in my sight because he hadn't had any drug or alcohol related addictions or even any theft and gambling habits and so, I had actually been quite surprised when the last strange, highly unusual, huge incident that I'd had to deal with as a hotel owner had involved him.

Quite unusually that day I had performed my building checks rather late in the day and in the middle of the afternoon instead of the morning but due to the decrease in guests and the influx of other problems, my routine had differed over that last few years due to all the legal complexities and visits to courtrooms, solicitors and lawyers that I'd had to contend with and to undertake. One of the other guests, a female guest called Queenie in her mid-fifties had grabbed my arm that afternoon as I had stepped onto the second-floor landing as I had walked around the building to perform my usual checks and then she had started to drag me towards the third floor.

"Mr. Gethin, you have to come straight away." Queenie had urged. "I think Alfie's going to jump. He shut himself inside his room yesterday and he won't come out or open the door to anyone and he won't speak to anyone."

Once I had arrived on the third floor and had knocked upon Alfie's door, I'd called out Alfie's name a few times but all I had been greeted with was total silence and so both Queenie and I had stood by his door for a few more minutes and she had even called out his name too as we had waited but Alfie had refused to speak to either of us. Despite the silence however, I had preserved as I'd continued to tap on his guest room door and call out his name repeatedly but after ten minutes there had been absolutely no response at all and so I had decided to take further action and to try and open his guest room door with the spare set of keys.

"I better go downstairs and get the spare key Queenie." I had explained just before I'd turned and then rushed back down to the ground floor and my office.

Just a few minutes later I had returned to the third floor with the spare key to Alfie's room but very strangely as I'd slipped the key inside the lock and then turned it to open the door, I had found that the door had not budged even an inch and as I'd leant upon it and pushed it, Alfie's door still hadn't moved even a centimeter.

"I think Alfie's pushed something heavy up against the door Queenie." I had concluded as I'd turned to face her. "It won't budge even an inch."

"We have to find a way to open it Mr. Gethin, I think he's going to jump out of the window or something." Queenie had urged. "He's been very down for the last few days and he said, he wasn't sure that he would be around anymore the last time I spoke to him. At first, I just thought that maybe they had found him somewhere permanent to live now or something like that but now I think he meant, he wanted to end his own life."

"Do you know what happened that might have made him feel that way?" I had asked.

"His girlfriend dumped him just a few days ago, she had someone else and I told him that many times but he never listened to me and he swore that they were going to live together and that she would move into his house once he was permanently rehoused." Queenie had replied. "He adored that woman and she barely even gave him a second glance, she never really gave a dam about him."

"Have you met her?" I had asked.

"Yes, just once though. I met them together on Camden High Street, she used to spend all his benefits as soon as he got paid." Queenie had said as she had shaken her head. "Because he had an injury from work, he was entitled to disability benefits which are slightly more and so she made sure that as soon as he got that money every fortnight, she spent every penny he had."

"That's not very nice of her." I had swiftly concluded.

"Well, she wasn't a very nice person, very materialistic and hard, a bit of money grabber if you ask me." Queenie had replied. "I did try to warn Alfie a few times but he wasn't having any of it, he just insisted that she loved him and that they were going to live together when he'd been rehoused."

"Did he tell you what happened that day?" I had asked.

"Yeah, he said that he caught her in the arms of her lover and that she ended it because he kicked up a fuss and threatened the man." Queenie had explained.

"Okay, I better call the emergency services." I had concluded. "You stay here please Queenie and just try to speak to him, see if you can get him to speak to you."

"Right, I'll do that Mr. Gethin." Queenie had immediately agreed. "I've been so worried about him really because I've knocked on his door about twenty times since yesterday and he hasn't answered once and usually, he answers me on the first knock."

"Don't worry Queenie, we'll have him out of there soon, I promise." I had reassured her.

Just a few seconds later I had turned and then headed back downstairs as I'd prepared to place an emergency call and to rescue Alfie from his depressed mental state. Every inch of my skin had trembled as I had walked towards the ground floor as I'd feared what might happen if the emergency services hadn't arrived in time but I had tried to keep calm because as I'd already known, if I had shown my alarm that wouldn't help anyone and especially not Queenie who had been very worried. One small comfort to me however, had been the fact that at least the incident hadn't involved some of the more troublesome guests that had resided in the hotel at that time and that from the handful of guests that had still remained upon the premises, Alfie and Queenie had both been by far the two most pleasant.

Approximately thirty minutes later two police officers and two fire fighters had arrived and so, I had quickly shown them up to the third floor and to Alfie's door and as they had inspected the door frame and the door, they'd discussed the best means of entry and a possible course of action. For a few minutes as I had waited for their suggestions and conclusions, I'd spoken to Queenie as I had checked what had happened since I'd left her and gone downstairs.

"Did you manage to get a response out Alfie yet Queenie?" I had asked.

"None at all Mr. Gethin, he won't even answer me never mind open the door and I've tried so many times now." Queenie had explained.

"Okay, I guess we'll just have to let the professionals handle it now. Don't worry Queenie, they know what they're doing, Alfie will be fine." I had reassured her.

Another few minutes had gone by as I had stood in total silence and just listened to the fire fighters and police officers speak and once they had agreed on a suitable course of action and discussed it with me, they had started to kick down the door.

"Don't come in here." Alfie had suddenly yelled at the top of his voice. "If you come in here, I'll jump."

One of the police officers at that point had turned to face me as they had both shaken their heads in total frustration and then he had started to ask both Queenie and myself some questions.

"Look Mr. Gethin, I know you are the owner of this hotel but who does Alfie speak to more? Who is he closer to between the two of you?" The police officer had asked.

"Definitely Queenie." I had replied.

"Okay Queenie, I'll need you to speak to Alfie, just tell him that everything is going to be fine and that you are here for him." The police officer had instructed her.

"Should I do anything?" I had asked.

"Yes, you can go and make Alfie a cup of tea and can you bring him some snacks please, anything that you have downstairs will do?" The police officer had advised. "If he's been in there since yesterday, he won't have eaten a thing and a hot drink might calm him down a bit."

"Right, I'll do that." I had immediately agreed.

"Good and then Queenie, you'll encourage Alfie to drink the cup of tea and to eat the snacks and that should move him away from the window and away from immediate danger."

The police officer had explained. "It's a very delicate situation and we don't want him to jump."

"How does Alfie normally take his tea Queenie?" I had asked as I'd turned to face her.

"He usually likes it with two sugars and milk Mr. Gethin." Queenie had replied.

"Okay, I'll sort that out for him now." I had reassured her.

"I think we're all done here George, we'll leave this crisis with you." One of the firemen had said as he had turned to face the second police officer.

"Yeah, you guys can go Dan. We'll handle things from here." The second police officer had agreed as he had nodded his head.

"Right, I'll see you guys out." I had offered.

Once I had satisfied myself that Alfie had been in safe hands, I'd begun to make my way back down towards the ground floor of the building with the two firemen in tow as I had escorted them back to the front door.

Approximately five minutes later and once I had found some snacks and made a hot cup of tea with a couple of spoonfuls of sugar in it and some milk, I'd returned to the third floor and the landing and much to my relief, Queenie had been in the middle of an actual conversation with Alfie, albeit through the broken door which he had actually wedged the bed up against and the wooden wardrobe.

"Here you go Queenie, try to get Alfie to drink this and to eat something." I had persuaded her as I'd handed her the cup of tea and the snacks.

"Yes, if he drinks and eats something that means there's hope." The first police officer had pointed out. "Ask him if he wants to come out or if you can slide them through the door."

"Right." Queenie had agreed as she had turned to face the door and had taken a deep breath. "Okay Alfie, I have a cup of tea here and it's just how you like it and there's some biscuits and even a slice of marble cake. Do you want to come out for them or should I slide them through the door to you?"

"Can you call an ambulance for me please?" The first police officer had asked as he'd turned to face me. "This is really a medical crisis. Just tell them that officers are on the scene and that they have requested an ambulance with medical responders."

"Okay, I'll go and do that now." I had agreed.

Approximately one hour later and a short while after the two medical responders had arrived and had then been shown up to the third floor, Alfie had finally been convinced to come out of the guest room and as I had walked everyone back downstairs, the two policemen and two medical responders had verbally encouraged Alfie as we had walked. When we had all arrived in the hallway, close to the hotel's front door, for a few minutes we'd all congregated close to the front door where the police officers and medical responders had held a quiet discussion at one side of the hallway for a couple of minutes, just before the four had prepared to depart.

"You know Alfie, you have a very nice friend here." The first police officer had said as he'd walked towards him and then had placed one of his hands upon his shoulder. "Queenie is a very good friend, she cares about you a lot, so you really shouldn't worry or get upset about people that don't."

"Yes, Queenie is a very good friend." Alfie had agreed as he'd nodded his head.

"And you're in good hands here." The police officer had mentioned. "People are looking out for you."

"I know." Alfie had agreed.

"Right, Mr. Gethin, we're going to leave now." The police officer had said as he had nodded his head. "We've had a discussion and we really think that it will be better for Alfie if he remains here with the people who care about him, besides hospital beds are very hard to get at the moment."

"I understand." I had replied.

"No more scares now Alfie, if you're upset about something talk to your friends about it, talk to the people that care about you." The police officer had encouraged he had tried to stabilize the situation. "Some women come and go like the wind and that one was just a very frosty, harsh gale that blew through your life like a storm. You can find someone else now because you are officially single, someone much nicer, someone that will really care about you."

"Mr. Gethin, I'll just pop out and get us all some fish and chips and when I come back, we can hang out in the lounge and play charades or cards or something." Queenie had suggested.

"Yeah why not." I had agreed as I'd nodded my head.

Just a minute or so later the police officers and medical responders had left and as Queenie had followed them out of the front door, I had taken Alfie gently by the arm and had then led him towards the small communal guest lounge. For the remainder of that evening and night, I had spent it with Queenie and Alfie as we'd eaten together, laughed together, drunk some beers and had even played some cards as the hours had slipped gently away for once, I'd pushed my own troubles aside and just focused on those around me as I had begun to appreciate their presence. Although I had been sent some truly awful, extremely difficult, very antisocial clients by Mike Walker over the years, it had been people like Queenie that had motivated and encouraged me because it had been people like Queenie that had made my hotel worth the while and that night had reminded me of that one sweetener when it had come to the issue of my increasingly difficult circumstances in life as I'd appreciated Queenie's kindness and had silently applauded her attitude of concern towards Alfie.

For the remainder of that year, I had watched as my hotel had become nothing more than just a legal battle and as the debts had grown and grown, I'd borrowed more and more money to comply with the legal regulations and to make essential repairs to the building. Although I had known that the hotel had been on its last breath and legs however, I'd continued to try and fight and had attempted to maneuver my way around the legal constraints but it had been virtually impossible because the bureaucratic strangleholds had been far too tight.

Technically by that point, I had almost owed as much money as the hotel itself had been worth and so, I'd definitely feared that when the awful day came that I had to sell the building which had no longer been something that I'd be able to avoid, I would be left penniless and destitute. The issue at that point had not been whether I could keep the hotel anymore but rather one of when it would be sold and if I would be able to walk away with any money at all, once all the debts had been settled because failure had crept up on me for decades and had silently wound its tentacles all around the hotel and so at that point, it had been ready to squeeze every last hope and breathe out of every wall of the hotel and out of me and to take everything that I had. Over those final years I had taken out some huge loans and they had been secured against the premises itself and the loans along with the legal fees incurred and the regulatory compliance fines had almost financially crippled me.

Slowly and surely, I had begun to wind

things down as I'd attempted to juggle the property and the debts and had emptied the hotel of clients because I had no longer been able to guarantee an accommodation provision to anyone and had even entered into an agreement to sell the building in an attempt to recoup some of the losses and to clear some of the debts. Inside the hotel as the building had become emptier and emptier, it had almost become like a morgue as the Happyvale Hotel had waited to be buried and finally laid to rest because all that had seemed to line the walls and that had echoed through the silent halls, landings and rooms had been the reminders of my failures and my every breath of defeat because defeat had been the only companion that had actually remained. Nothing but an eerie silence had blanketed and enveloped the building which had hung in the air, present not just inside each of the guest rooms but also in the communal areas which had seemed so strange for me at the time because for so many years, the walls of those rooms had been decorated with so much hectic drama, chaotic shenanigans, loud shrieks, hearty laughter, angry shouts, tears of heartbreak and the hysterical antics of those who had occupied the hotel's interior.

Since the building had no longer required a cleaner, Ursula had been let go at around that time as I had fully surrendered and had totally accepted my defeat but she had been released with a heavy heart because although at times she had been sloppy and careless, over the years she had definitely been more of a supportive help to me than an actual hindrance. On so many occasions Ursula had definitely provided me with an essential crutch of support and a strong shoulder to lean upon when I had struggled to walk through life and when I'd been swamped by the swarm of troubles that had infested and invaded every possible inch of the hotel's interior and exterior and so as I had released Ursula from her employment duties, I'd felt saddened and as if somehow, I had failed not just myself but also Ursula too.

Finally, the inevitable and foreseeable had happened and so I'd had to pack up my bags and then leave the hotel that I'd grown up in and that I had lived in all my life because I'd placed the building in someone else's hands and name via a sale in order to settle the huge debts because all my legal maneuvers had yielded absolutely nothing for me but even more debt. My departure hadn't been pretty and there had been absolutely no saving graces or financial rewards in the end but at least I had been able to find a small grain of comfort in the fact that I hadn't left without a fight, I couldn't, I'd owed it to my mother who had devoted so much of her life to the building that I had grown up in, to at least try to keep the hotel alive and her legacy.

In so many ways, I had felt as if I'd failed, I had failed my mother who had obviously had more faith in my than I'd had in myself, I had failed myself in that I'd been handed something so valuable by the woman that had been the heart and center of my world and who I had loved so much and I'd totally screwed it up, due to my lack of knowledge, experience and skills. My life, I now realize had never been set in stone like some other people's lives in that they often had hopes and aspirations that they had then striven and had worked to achieve and I had never ever been naturally been gifted, particularly clever or drawn towards a particular profession, vocation or career. When it came to my attitude towards life, I had never been a great risk taker that had liked to live on the edge and I'd never had any great lightning bolts of ingenuity and so, the hotel really had been the only real chance for me to achieve something in life but as I now realize, fate writes our future and we either step up to succeed or stumble and tumble down the slippery slope of failure as we participate in life.

Throughout the twenty-five years of my hotel ownership I had made heaps and heaps of mistakes, I'd taken so much for granted, I had failed to see how much hard work had that responsibility had required and I'd definitely failed to appreciate the huge opportunity that had been given to me from all my mother's tireless hard work and those deep regrets still live within me to this very day. The bureaucratic processes involved with the hotel's ownership had baffled and confused me and I had definitely not totally understood the full implications of the responsibility that I'd taken on and although I had struggled for so many years, finally my ignorance, my shortfalls of experience, my lack of wisdom, a lack of reliable trustworthy support and my misplaced trust had been my own downfall as the hotel had slipped from my hands and I'd been left with nothing but just painful memories of my failure and my empty heartbroken regrets.

Over twenty-five years had gone by since I had first stepped through the Happyvale Hotel's front door as the hotel's owner and most of those years, the hotel had verged on the brink of collapse, clamped firmly between the walls of total disaster and absolute mess but for the most part at least, I'd definitely stuck the distance because I had never imagined throughout my younger years that I'd ever be responsible one day for an actual hotel. My ownership of the Happyvale Hotel had been nothing more in the end than a total wreckage with nothing but mangled carnage to leave behind as I had walked away totally destitute, absolutely penniless and with just the debris of my broken heart which had been full of heartbroken regrets and heartbeats of painful failure. Only one small comfort and consolation had really remained for me and I hold onto that even now because the fact that I had run the marathon of life with the hotel in my hands and that I'd kept the hotel's doors open for so very long, I had definitely felt had been some kind of achievement for a boy that had never been expected to achieve anything in life and for a boy that had never been expected to amount to anything much at all.

Printed in Great Britain
by Amazon